HEXES, HIGHBALLS & HOCKEY

A Charmed Cocktail Cozy

M.L. BONATCH

Cover Art by Spellbinding Designs

Editor: Three Point Author Services

Proofreader: Y.K. Bonatch

HEXES, HIGHBALLS & HOCKEY

When my specialty drink was returned for the second time, it was time to intervene. The frilly cocktail waitress dress swayed with the swing of my hips.

"Is there something wrong with the drink?" I eyed the slender mortal man who'd been brave enough to approach gin-and-juice Gloria, Night Moves queen customer complainer and mega witch. The later club hours tended to deter mortals, when the supernatural folk let their glamour fade. Mortals realized magic existed, but they were only willing to stray so far from their reality.

The man shook his head while leaning to see past me. "I was hoping to talk to the bartender." He lifted his drink with a shaky hand, rattling the ice cubes.

I relaxed. It wasn't my drink. "Listen ..."

"Steve."

"Well, Steve, Burton's busy." Usually as long as the mortals minded their own business, the paranormal minded theirs, but throw in too much booze, and there were often poor decisions, and a lot of cleaning up and explaining to do.

"You wouldn't understand. You're not a mortal." The man ran his gaze over my hair, settling on the black streak.

Mortals didn't have to worry about a misspell showing up as a black streak like witches did. I envied the uniform coloring of his perfect coif. My misguided spelling attempts had left my hair with a shameful streak and a lot of frizz to advertise my magical mistakes. "The drink was okay, then?"

"The best highball I ever had. If he won't come over, can I go talk to him?" He stood, swaying on his feet.

I braced a hand on his chest to steady him and pause his pursuit. "Only if you're going to ask him which tequila he recommends." I didn't want to scare this guy, but he needed to be scared. Burton was my friend in a warped kind of way, but he was also a demon.

The guy's eyes widened, and a twinge of sobriety must've made him pause. "Will he send me to hell?"

"Sugar, look around. You're already there." I held out my arms to encompass the club. "Do you see anything else here besides monsters?" With a flick of my finger, I let the glamour fall away. It was easy to accept that weres, vamps, witches, and about every other creature under the sun were mixed in among the mortals when they looked almost like everyone else. It wasn't easy when you got a glimpse of their true nature.

I dropped my arms and let the curtain of glamour return to cloak the club. The dude's face paled, and my quick reflexes caught his glass before it hit the floor. A few ice cubes toppled over the side.

Grace came to stand beside me as we watched him stumble toward the door. "Marissa Hale, did you scare another customer away?"

I'd done it before, when a patron got too drunk, or annoying. Grace just didn't know this one was being too stupid. "At least he had already paid his tab before leaving."

Grace folded her arms over the tray she clutched against her chest. "Burton's not going to be happy."

I shrugged. "It's not like you can tell. Burton doesn't seem to have any emotions." I picked the cash off the table and counted it. "Besides, this guy left a hefty tip." I handed her half.

"See, and people say you have no real heart."

Grace draped her arm around my waist. Her height prevented her from reaching my shoulders.

"They don't give me enough credit. Make sure you put in a good word with my sister. Ava never believes that I have the best intentions." My twin sister, Ava, was the better person out of the two of us and was temporarily here in Florida for work.

Grace looked to me. "Do you have plans for your day off tomorrow?"

I scoured my brain. There had to be something better to say than a big fat nothing after my hair appointment with Joe other than returning to the Willow Hill witch and warlock retirement condominium where I lived with Gran.

But with Gran off on a cruise, those retired busybodies were far too interested in the shenanigans that seemed to follow me. Especially since one of the first things I did after starting this job was find a dead body. Then a charmed cocktail gone rogue somehow gave me the ability to talk to Jasper, the stray cat I was forced to adopt. I had to. He wouldn't shut up until I did. Plus, he was kind of cute, although Mulder, my Shih Tzu, wasn't keen on the addition. "Umm, not yet."

"Great! Brian came down with something, so you can go to the hockey game with me."

Grace hurried away because she knew I would refuse. Not only because I preferred talking to animals or oldsters over anyone else, but also because I had no interest in hockey. But I didn't want to let her down, either. "Sure. Why not."

❧

"THANK THE GODDESS THEY HAVE PULLED PORK nachos, or I would've flipped my lid." That was a slight exaggeration. It would've taken a demon setting my feet on fire for me to consider removing the autographed Bayo Banshees hockey team cotton twill hat my hairstylist, Joe, had loaned me. It barely contained my frazzled mass of pink curls.

"No one else would've gotten me to agree to go to a hockey game besides you, Grace." I settled into the cramped arena seat and placed the plastic tray on my lap, folding my elbows against my sides to avoid jamming them into my neighbors.

Grace smiled apologetically at the werewolf I had bumped on my right. "Don't mind Marissa. It's her first hockey game."

I knew nothing about hockey—nor did I care to —and barely recognized my coworker out of her Night Moves uniform. The bulky jersey swallowed up her petite frame. Grace was decked out in team merchandise from the pristine ball cap on her head to her sneaker laces with the Bayo Banshee black and blue team colors.

My sigh had failed to gain her attention. "You could've taken me up on my offer to stir up one of my get-well-soon remedy spells for Brian."

"You know I love my boyfriend." Grace's gaze was locked on the players warming up on the ice.

I shrugged. "Hey, I offered." She knew me well enough to refuse. Besides hair care, magical medicine was one of my weak spelling areas.

"*Broken broomsticks!* I forgot to grab extra napkins." I stood, eager for an excuse to escape the confines of the tiny space. It didn't help that the overabundance of flesh that was the huge werewolf next to me kept spilling into my meager—and now non-existent—personal space. I wrinkled my nose. He smelled as if he hadn't bathed since the last full moon, although the odor could've been from his rumpled jersey.

Grace had babbled about extraordinarily specific washing instructions and superstitions about bad luck resulting from not caring for a team jersey appropriately. That was right after her enthusiasm had overridden her practical nature and she'd insisted I borrow one of hers, something I believed she now immensely regretted, based on her expression when I bought the nachos.

"Sit down." Grace tugged on the oversized jersey until I flopped into the seat and almost doused myself with nacho cheese. "The game's about to start." Her eager smile lit her dark brown eyes. "It's bad manners to get up until a break between plays. Besides, I have a few extra napkins."

Of course, she did. My ruse to return to the bar area to hang out was squelched. "There seem to be a lot of rules and etiquette attached to being a spectator."

"You'll like it, you'll see." She nudged me, offering a mound of napkins large enough to blanket myself, confirming she didn't trust me eating while wearing her jersey.

"If you say so. Now stop worrying. I can spell out a stain better than anyone." I jammed a tortilla chip teetering with delicious mounds of pork, cheese, and barbecue sauce into my mouth.

Grace blinked and appeared stricken at my comment. She shook her head. The tiny Banshee logo earrings dangling from her lobes swung back and forth as if struggling to take flight. She met the withering stare of the were on my right. "She's a newbie."

After clearing her throat, she spoke loud enough for the glaring werewolf to overhear. "Marissa, there's no spelling in the hockey game or the arena. *Nothing*. No magic. It's against the rules. The players are mixed—supernatural and mortal. Using any kind of magic or paranormal skills will get a player fined, or worse. Plus, the Supernatural Hockey League—the SHL—would boot them from the team. Nothing is permitted to be charmed by the spectators, or the players, so it's a fair game." She nodded after finishing what sounded like something recited word for word from the player's rulebook. Knowing Grace, it probably was.

"No magic?" I frowned around a mouthful of chips. More rules to add to Grace's ever-growing list. "What's the use of having a skill if you aren't allowed to use it?" Ava would've backed me on this. She was always on the lookout for discrimination against witches. It wasn't as if the werewolves weren't benefitting from their immense physical stature, and the vampires' speed permitted them to race across the ice with lightning speed.

A few tortilla crumbs dribbled from my lips and clung to her cherished jersey. I quickly brushed them away and brought up a question to distract her from noticing the stray morsels. "Tell me again why I'm going to like sitting in an icebox watching a bunch of men pummel each other over a plastic doodad."

Her eyes lit up, but before she could speak, the

announcer bellowed something about the game starting. Grace and the were both jumped to their feet. Unprepared for the jostling and onslaught of surrounding elbows, I dropped the sopping tortilla chip.

The cheese and barbecue-covered chunks of pork oozed onto the jersey. *Rusty cauldrons!* I tried to blot the mess before Grace noticed. My efforts at wiping only made the stain worse. The large Banshee image sewn on the front of the jersey morphed from raging to repulsive.

After ensuring her attention was fixed on player number sixty-nine hustling down the ice, I focused on the mess. Surely a teeny, tiny spell won't show up on the radar? Heck, the wrath of the magic-hating SHL would surely have been less than Grace's if she discovered the stain. The smeared, clotting cheese was rapidly giving the jersey the appearance of a napkin.

I glanced at Grace. The roar of the crowd made it unnecessary to mutter the enchanted words under my breath, but I did anyway. My furtive glances assured me she didn't notice the mess, or the magic.

Grace jostled Joe's beloved hat as she tested the boundaries of her seating area with flailing arms when the announcer identified the players. "Hey, watch the hat." I grabbed the hat to steady it and contain my compressed curls as I finished the spell. A small shimmery cloud circled the congealing cheese. As the cloud dissipated, so did the cheese. I smiled as the Banshee returned to looking nasty instead of nauseous. "That should do the trick."

A tingling on my scalp and a tightening of my curls validated the processing of the spell, and further deteriorated the meager work Joe had performed on my locks. I could already hear his remarks at the damage I had just inflicted to my tresses. But a witch had to do what a witch had to do.

After ensuring the jersey appeared as good as new, and then finishing my nachos before the big boy beside me elbowed me again, I settled in to see why Grace was always fussed up about hockey.

My attention locked on the player with the number sixty-nine jersey, who'd flashed repeatedly on the screen, as he performed admirable hockey plays. The players all looked the same to me with their matching helmets, jerseys, and pads. The only reason I noticed it was the same dude was because his number had made me chuckle ... and his last name was Sexton.

I might've been a full-grown adult witch at twenty-eight, but my sense of humor often channeled a fifteen-year-old pubescent boy. I giggled. "How's that for a name and number? Does he go by Mr. Sexy?"

Grace ignored my comment as she focused on Mr. Sexy racing down the ice toward the prized net. "He's a rookie, but tonight," her gaze became wistful, "it's like he's a different player. He's playing so well, it's almost like he's spelled."

I tensed but relaxed again when her focus remained on the ice, not me. Cleaning up the nacho cheese had been a little spell. No harm done.

A horn blared and the music began again. "Hey, watch it!" I stood to avoid being assaulted by Grace and my neighbor's butt as they gyrated to the beat. I didn't know what was going on, but dancing was always a good idea. Especially after the once again pristine borrowed jersey assured me I'd narrowly avoided my friend's legendary wrath. "I love this song."

"Throw your hat." Grace tossed her hat to sail through the air and join the others littering the ice. She elbowed me when I ignored her.

"What? No way. You've seen what my hair looks like." She'd listened to me complain the whole way here about how I had to leave before Joe could finish. "Plus, Joe will kill me if I lose his hat."

"You have to throw it. Sexton got three goals.

That's called a hat trick!" She tugged at my hat. "Fans are supposed to throw their hats on the ice."

"That's nice." I clutched the hat while she tugged. "I'm not a fan yet."

Grace ignored my pleas and grimaced once she freed my monstrosity of curls, seeming to rethink her decision, but followed through and tossed the hat.

"Witch, don't tell me you saved this hot mess for me." Joe lifted my mass of curls and let the strands fall to my shoulders.

"Okay, I won't." I winced, hoping to avoid the attention of the other clientele at Super Strands. Each spell I cast enhanced my curls until they morphed into coils wild enough to turn medusa to stone. Last night's jersey spell undid Joe's recent work.

"Where's the hat I loaned you?"

"About that ..."

His humor faded. "Don't tell me you lost my autographed Bayo Banshees hat." He laid a hand on my head and narrowed his eyes, reminding me without a word that hats could become an essential part of my wardrobe.

"No, I didn't lose it." The desperate lie stumbled from my lips. Surely, I could get the hat back. I'd ask Grace. "I left it at home."

"Ms. Marissa ..." He cocked his hand on his hip. "It almost seems as though you've gone and done another spell. But even I know you wouldn't be foolish enough to enchant *anything* at a hockey game." He raised a perfectly plucked brow and waited for my lame excuse. Joe was paid more pennies than I'd ever see, had a head as bald as a cue ball, and he took hair care seriously.

"Of course not." It wasn't really a lie. Surely such a tiny spell didn't count. "It's just that I can't afford to come as often as I'd like." Joe could only squeeze me into a cancellation slot when I got a big tip, and finagling that tip often walked the line of risking my job. I'd yet to get permission to serve my charmed cocktails, even though many patrons requested them. Once in a while, I could be convinced to prepare one for the clientele I liked, and occasionally, for those I didn't care for.

He rolled his eyes, but not before the spark of the challenge lit his dark, almond-shaped peepers. "I'll see what I can do. I'm a beautician, not a magician."

"The magic you work on my hair makes me beg to

differ." I offered my most apologetic smile. Compliments got me everywhere with Joe. He pursed his lips and got to work.

Truth be told, no one was quite sure what Joe was. I had my bet set on witch, but I might've been biased, wanting to have the eccentric, trash-talker on my team. He managed my hair as if he utilized a spell, but he might've just been that awesome at styling.

Others felt the way in which he rocked any wig or outfit meant he was a vampire—those centuries-old divas never lost their style. A few still insisted he must've been some sort of shifter, since his appearance was never the same twice. Regardless, I was happy he liked, or at least tolerated, me.

"One day I hope you'll share your secret." Then maybe I could tweak out the shades of suspicious spelling myself.

"I've explained the process."

"But I could never replicate it." I told myself he wasn't telling me all his secrets because he liked my company and didn't want me to start shirking appointments. "I guess being a hairdresser is an art."

"You know it." He squeezed my shoulders, reveling in the compliment.

I laid one hand on top of his. Joe treated me with the same high-class sarcastic care as any other salon client. They weren't all unkind, just the few that recognized me from the club. I knew most of the faces under the dryers and knew many of their names —and their signature drink—but most didn't know mine. I was 'girl' or 'bartender' or 'honey.'

From the mirror I spotted a few of them gazing at me now, acting as if I was here to deliver their drinks even though I wasn't wearing my cocktail dress. Scotch-and-a-side-of-Valium Cindy muttered that the trash was starting to stink. It didn't take an insight spell to know she was referring to me.

"They aren't going to let me forget I don't belong here. Especially since I know more than one of their shady secrets." After a few too many cocktails, supernatural abilities or not, most lips and tails started wagging. More than one of my potent drinks stirred with a touch of a spell often spilled skeletons out of a closet. Not my intent, but a fortunate—or unfortunate, depending on how you looked at it—side-effect.

Joe followed my gaze. "I say who sits in my chair and who doesn't."

When his voice rose at the end of the sentence, Cindy busied herself with a magazine.

"Thanks, Joe."

"What occasion got you to a sporting event?" He studied my reflection which looked as out of place in the posh salon as a paper umbrella gracing a whiskey on the rocks. Unlike Joe, I was incapable of mixing harsh borrowed femininity with finesse.

I sighed and dropped my gaze from the mirror when I detected vodka-and-tonic Tina's toxic glare fixed on me after I had focused on her bodacious bosom. She probably regretted that last drink the other night when she inadvertently blathered on about her recent supernatural enhancements. "It's called the hazards of being a friend."

"Big men with long sticks aren't your thing, then?" Joe strutted in his stilettos to snag a tube of product from the counter. The gold-colored cylinder promising eloquent, sleek locks farted in trailer trash protest as he squeezed it to fill his palm with questionable goop.

"I didn't say that. Why, are they *your* thing?" I smiled. We'd played this game since the day we had met. I think he liked that I challenged him like no one else dared.

"Um, umm, it's going to take a few hours to get your hair to stop misbehaving." He winked and glanced at his enviable profile.

"You didn't answer my question." I didn't know any more about whether he considered himself a man or a woman, or what the nature of his sexual preference was, any more than I knew his placement in the supernatural family tree. He was a mystery.

Joe turned up the music at his station, irking the other hairdressers stationed nearby. They preferred the relaxing melodies tinkling overhead to the pop music he bobbed to while working in his personal space. None of them dared complain. His tongue was sharper than any pair of shears.

"A few hours? I don't have that long." The clock was ticking, and I couldn't afford that much of his time.

"Well, girl, then you're going to have to leave with my masterpiece incomplete." He gestured to the spot on my head where he'd begun to straighten my hair. Half of my hair was a lustrous, sleek, enviable pink, while the rest appeared like the result of sticking my finger in a light socket.

"I can't go to work looking like this." My shrill tone drew the attention of the werewolves who had sensitive hearing, including one who I didn't want to notice me—none other than the owner, Frederick Kaynine. He'd warned me more than once about disturbing his customers in the peaceful salon environment. I couldn't help my loud, robust nature any more than he could ignore the phases of the moon. It was just who I was. But who I was, and what I was, irritated some more than others. The macho wolf acted as if witches were homing in on his hairy territory like an eighties hair band.

"Seriously, Joe?" Every witch would sneer at my unfinished afro, as it blatantly blasted the truth about my lack of spelling skill. The largest sinister-looking streak had expanded courtesy of the charmed cocktail that had backfired and given me the unusual ability to talk with my cat. Many assumed I had stirred a spell of nasty intent, but it hadn't been a bad spell; I was just bad at spelling.

"You should've remembered my hat." Joe spun on a heel and snagged a hat from a shifter passing by who had come into the shop with a delivery of hair products. He jammed it over my masses of curls and bent to meet my distressed gaze in the mirror to wink. "Tell your sister I said hello."

I touched the hat, hesitating on the spot where the dark streak lay hidden.

A flicker of sympathy—or indigestion from the teeny tiny fancy appetizers he grazed on all day—crossed Joe's face as he studied my exaggerated pout. "Fine."

He scrolled through the calendar at his station, tilting it so I could see the client appointment he indicated. "Misty's last tip wouldn't cover the cost of cheese on a cracker. There might be an opening coming up in my schedule."

"Hexed!"

I tensed and scanned the bar to try to determine who had shouted the word that evoked a witches' ire faster than hair grew on a werewolf. The accusatory chant had originated from the television. I frowned and stepped closer to the screen. A reporter stood in front of the arena Grace and I had visited a few nights ago. The street bum still commandeering the corner with his plethora of hodgepodge possessions confirmed the hockey arena as one and the same. I called out to Burton, "Can you turn the television up, please?"

I focused on the screen. The impeccably smooth porcelain skin identified the reporter as a vamp. HIs eyes sparkled as he announced the accusatory allegations. Vamps were always eager to share unsavory stories about supernatural species other than their own. Most reporters were vampires, since news tended to break from dusk to dawn in a community thriving with supernatural sorts.

One corner of the screen displayed the camera panning the arena crowd the night of the game, searching for signs of spelling. Apparently, the Supernatural Hockey League had already started their investigation. I recognized our seats by the large advertisement that had been behind us. As the camera panned past, I leaned in with anticipation.

Hopefully I wouldn't be in the process of shoveling in nachos.

No need to worry. I was obscured by Grace's exuberant gestures over a hockey play and the massive were beside me. So much for my five seconds of fame.

Another sweep of the spectators brought up the familiar face of the guy who I'd chased off the other night—Steve. The image of the reporter overtook the screen and he babbled on about the investigation. Onlookers on the screen from the opposing team shouted for the referees to review the game to rule out magic interference. Then the player and the witch could be dealt with accordingly.

The player's photo was displayed. He was muscular enough to be a were, gorgeous enough to be a vamp, all while maintaining the natural look attributed to mortals. I squirmed when the number sixty-nine and the name Sullivan "Sully" Sexton popped up beside him with the headline, *Was the hockey game hexed?*

I rolled my eyes. Of course, blame the skill he displayed during that game on magic. The humiliating memory of losing Joe's hat and leaving the arena under scrutinizing stares still haunted me. There would be a lot more staring if I couldn't retrieve Joe's hat and he banned me from the salon.

I reflexively reached for my hair, which I'd tamed the extra frizz from the recent jersey spell into a twist. I gasped and looked back to the screen. The news had moved on to another story. But I'd suddenly been hit with a terrifying thought. Surely the spell to save Grace's jersey, and my butt from her wrath, had nothing to do with that hockey investigation?

I scanned the club for Burton. While others pondered what emotions lurked behind his flat façade, I welcomed someone who at least pretended to be interested in other people more than himself. Whether he actually listened or not remained uncertain. But one thing I was certain of was Burton's obsession with hockey. When Grace prattled on about some hockey thing or another, his expression became slightly animated. He would let me know if I should start panicking about the teeny, tiny spell.

"So, Burton, remember the hockey game I went to with Grace?" I took a deep breath, preparing to blurt it out before changing my mind. "I might've accidentally cast a little spell to get rid of a stain on Grace's jersey. You know how she is about her jersey. I'm sure it has nothing to do with whatever nonsense they're talking about on television. Right?" I glanced at him. His attention veered to me, and his brows rose the slightest bit as a flash of red crossed his eyes.

Darn. It was worse than I thought.

I was hoping for a total lack of response. The last time I got the minuscule brow raise was when I spelled the hand dryer in the ladies' bathroom . Years of magic advancements, and still no one could make a dryer work well enough to avoid resorting to hand towels and tissues? Those often ended up on the floor and then some poor waitress—usually me—had to pick up the used paper.

My good intentions had accidentally blown up the hand dryer—which had, in turn, taken out the entire wall—while some ladies had still been using the toilets. And the club had happened to be full. I cringed recalling the outrage. Apparently, some secrets were more coveted than others. Ladies' toileting habits being one of them. It took all my charm, and a lot of persuading, to keep my job.

Speaking of jobs, the increasing noise volume in the club warned me that I'd better get moving. No use panicking about what they might, or might not, determine about the hockey game. I rolled my shoulders, shaking off my tension. No use panicking—yet.

❧ 3 ❧

The club was so busy that I didn't have a chance to give the nacho cheese spell another thought for most of the evening. I tugged at the skirt hemline of my Night Moves uniform. The eloquent line of the dress was lost on me since it was as uncomfortable as were hair on a Fae or like the aforementioned were had gotten fleas.

I ducked to avoid gin-and-juice Gloria's glare. That witch always seemed to sit at my table. Serving her one of my specialty cocktails the first time she'd come to the club had been a mistake, because then she kept coming back. She was more of a pain than my aching feet. She always sat alone in a corner table with her back to the wall, always asked for me, and was positively unbearable.

I felt a presence behind me as a large shadow cast over mine. I sighed. "I know."

"She's getting impatient." Burton's deep voice carried over my shoulder. I turned, but he stared past me with his usual emotionless expression as he surveyed the club. To most, he was more of an oddity and enigma than the rest of the eccentric array of supernatural species frequenting the club, but to me, he was just Burton.

I braced a hand on my hip. "It's only been five minutes. That woman has been around for a bajillion years. Five minutes should be nothing to her."

"That's not the point."

I rolled my eyes. I knew what the point was, or should I say, whose pointy teeth insisted I give old Gloria extra attention. The big boss, Vlad.

At first I thought it was because she gave so much money to the club, mainly in the form of patronizing it all the time, but I was starting to think it was something more. A witch with full ebony hair meant she didn't give a crapola about who or what she spelled, or the consequences.

"I'm going." When I glanced to her table our eyes locked. Darn it, she'd already seen me. I gestured that I was getting her drink and then squeezed past the tree trunk rooted behind me that was Burton. "I'll get it. She likes my mix."

I rushed behind the bar before Burton could intercept me and make the drink—or see my extra secret ingredient. Before she could throw another stink eye, I arrived at her table with her drink and a sweet smile.

"It took you long enough. Hasn't Vlad taught you about keeping the customers happy? Perhaps I'll have to remind him." Gloria looked almost as old as Vlad, and despite being a witch, she had that old-school vamp black-as-night hair and pale-as-death skin with a skeletal frame to match.

When she narrowed her eyes, the little twinge of guilt I'd been feeling from spiking her drink dissipated. "I'm sorry." *I wasn't.*

I set the drink down in front of her and waited. She shook her mane of hair. It glistened as if the darkness within her had leaked to gather in her locks with all the bad magic she'd performed. Her fair, weathered completion indicated she may have started as a blonde. I imagined her eyes used to be an icy blue but faded to the gray of an overcast day, as if any spark of joy had been extinguished.

She lifted the glass to her lips but didn't drink. "I'll keep my hair appointment tomorrow."

"What?" I struggled to conceal my surprise. Perhaps it was a coincidence. Or she was talking out loud about her hair appointment as if we were having a conversation and it wasn't just her demanding a drink and me pretending I was happy to get it.

"The one you're trying to spell my drink to get." She arched a thin brow.

"I don't know what you're talking about." But oh, I did, and in all these years, not one witch had ever caught on. I was only trying to soften her harshness to a more tolerable level.

Gloria's expression said she knew that I knew exactly what she was talking about. "Fool me once, shame on you. Fool me twice, shame on me. Fool me —there's never a third time."

Her words hung heavy and threatening. I got the feeling she was talking about more than the drink. She had some major anger issues buried under all that black hair, and I didn't want to find out what they were.

"Don't worry. I'm not going to report you. Not if you make me another drink better and faster this time." She batted her hand at me as if I were an annoying insect. "Actually, I kind of admire your passive-aggressive ruthlessness. Even if it's a little entitled. You should consider what witch you cross when you're stirring unsolicited charmed cocktails."

"What ... How ..." I snapped my trap shut. Every word was an admission of guilt, so silence was the best response. If the drink was examined closely, it would show up as charmed. That in itself wasn't the issue; it was because she hadn't asked for the charm—and Vlad still hadn't given me permission to charm cocktails without oversight.

"Easy. I saw it." She pulled her eyelid wide with her bony fingers until the glass eyeball fell from the socket.

I grimaced. Disgusting.

She held the glass eyeball on her palm, and it rotated, taking in the scenery. I struggled to keep myself from gaping. Then she held the eyeball over the drink and dropped it in with a *plop*.

I jumped when the liquid splattered my hand.

The ice-blue color of the lone iris pressed against the side of the glass to peer out before the freakish orb receded behind the ice cubes to spin around, bumping the sides of the glass.

"What the—" I'd seen some weird stuff in my years, but nothing came close to this freakish eyeball staring at me from amongst the cubes.

Gloria fished out the dripping eyeball. She stared at me with one eye and an empty sunken-in socket closed. She pulled open the vacant socket and held her hand beneath it with her open palm. The glass eyeball wiggled across her fingers, leaving a trail of moisture from the gin and juice in its wake like some kind of un-housebroken pet. A popping sound startled me as the eye wiggled back in place in the socket.

Gloria studied me with her one semi-normal eye while the other one still displayed its white underside, devoid of color. The eye shimmied and moved around in the socket until the iris was facing outward. She blinked and then opened both eyes with a smile. "There. I don't want to freak anyone out."

Too late for that. I'd never be able to mix a highball again without a visual of that eyeball.

The best tactic now was to play stupid and not ask about her weird pet eyeball that tasted her drinks and could detect a magic potion. That was some freaky stuff, and it made me uncomfortable that she might've had other tricks up her sleeve—or falling out with another body part. "You don't like your drink." My wide smile felt strained. "Let me get you another one." I picked up the glass and ignored her earlier comments.

"Don't take so long this time. I've got my eye on you."

I planned to avoid speaking with Gloria for the rest of the shift and deliver her strong drinks swiftly and spell-free. Hopefully Burton would intervene if she decided to retaliate with a spell of her own.

"Where's Grace?" I peered around Samantha as if the towering, willowy waitress might've been blocking my friend. I wanted to ask Grace how to get Joe's hat back. If she confirmed there was no possible way, like Burton claimed when I'd asked him, then plan B was to convince her to take me to another game. Where there was a will and a determined witch who valued the skills of a sarcastic but spectacular hairdresser, there was a way to recover a cruddy, old hat.

Samantha was checking her profile with a small mirror while leaning against the bar. The gorgeous, cold-blooded folks incessantly gazed at their likeness as if fearing the old myth might come true any minute and they'd no longer reflect. I restrained myself from commenting on her overabundance of vanity. As a vampire, she always looked fabulous. I should know; she was my chief competition for tips. I had to make up for what I lacked in looks with better drinks. By "better," I meant strong enough to take the hair off a were, or perhaps a charmed cocktail.

"We switched shifts. She went to the hockey game." Samantha tucked the mirror into her apron pocket.

"There's another hockey game?" Those guys spent more time playing hockey than a vamp did preening.

Samantha shrugged. "I guess. I hope the players stop by again. They give the best tips. Plus, those boys are amazing eye candy."

She walked away, still smiling as if envisioning the players padding her pockets—and perhaps more. I frowned, realizing I'd have to determine another way to retrieve Joe's hat or find another one.

"Oh, my goddess."

I might've ignored Samantha's exclamation, thinking a rogue hair had drawn her concern, if it weren't for Burton's sharp intake of breath. I followed their gaze to the television.

The camera panned past the bum nesting in front of the arena. A plethora of junk overflowed his shopping cart.

"Well, Darn." He was wearing Joe's missing hat. The inscription on the brim was barely legible, but the way the *O* in Joe's name was transformed into a smiley face with devil horns confirmed it. Unfortunately, the stolen hat wasn't what the news crew was interested in, and it was the least of my worries.

"Oh, no." She may have hung her head while the cameras whirred, snapping photos, but Grace's face was unmistakable. Brian trailed behind with a befuddled expression as they led her from the arena with her hands behind her in magic binding cuffs. Grace's meek, mild demeanor no doubt had Brian wondering —like me—what she could've possibly done to get arrested. This had to be a mistake.

I strained to hear the reporter, but a loud rock

video suddenly appeared on the screen. "Hey." I shot Burton an accusatory glare. He nodded toward the door. The big boss had just ambled in. Burton was trying to preserve Grace's job.

Vlad, the head honcho vamp of the club, had little tolerance for witches, let alone ones that worked for him and got publicly arrested on television. Innocent or not, it was unlikely he wanted that kind of press. It would provide him with the perfect excuse to fire a witch without risking accusations of discrimination. He could insist the bad press might hurt business.

I rushed over to the bar and whispered to Burton. "Did they say what happened?"

Before Burton could answer, or even blink, Samantha with her advanced vamp hearing piped in. "Apparently when Grace entered the arena through the magic detectors, she set off the alarms. There was magic residue on her jersey." Her eyes widened enough to emphasize her predatory pupils. "The SHL has to rule out that Grace isn't responsible for the alleged hockey hex at the game the other night."

"No." I met Burton's knowing stare. There was a mistake. We knew who was responsible, and it wasn't Grace.

Samantha leaned in, eager to hold my attention. "You know how witches love to meddle with magic."

She paused and ran her gaze over me. "No offense, but I bet it was Grace. You know how obsessed she is with that hockey stuff."

Samantha brimmed with too much annoying enthusiasm at Grace's expense. The vamp reveled in dishing gossip about anyone other than her. She glanced toward where Vlad was ducking into his office. No doubt she was eager to tell him about Grace, to divert his attention from her own recent scandal that had almost gotten her suspended.

"Don't even think about it," I said, emphasizing each word enough to gain Samantha's attention and temper her excitement. "It's all hearsay. Nothing to get the boss riled up about." I tilted my head and narrowed my eyes. "Unless, of course, you want me to share what I heard about whiskey-on-the-rocks Wally. You know—the guy you were draping yourself all over the other night. Lisa's husband."

"That's all lies. Lisa's jealous," Samantha raised her voice as if to convince herself of her own innocence.

Her glancing away from my accusatory stare was all the confirmation of guilt I needed. Lisa was yet another wife intent on having Samantha fired and her hide turned into a doormat due to the scandalous rumors about the cocktail waitress and her husband.

"Just rumors, then? Oh, if bathroom walls could

talk. And in fact, for me, they could if I asked." My smile was slow. "Because, you know, I'm a witch. You know how us witches love to meddle with magic." Samantha had less knowledge and understanding about magic than my pinky finger. I could tell her anything I wanted about the craft, and she'd choke on it hook, line, and sinker.

If Samantha's skin could pale any further, she would've become transparent. "You can't do that," she said with little conviction, doubt crossing her porcelain features.

"I can. But I won't, if you leave Grace out of it. And while you're at it, how about having something nice to say about witches occasionally?" I wiggled my fingers as if I were about to cast a spell.

She grabbed her drink tray and sped away. My hair rose and fell with the gust of her hasty departure. Perhaps I should've went to see what those walls had to say—the information might've come in handy. Or maybe not. There were some things you couldn't un-hear.

"You shouldn't feed her fear." Burton stared at me with his unreadable features.

"She deserved it." Perhaps I was partially responsible for Samantha's discomfort with witches, but she'd made her feelings clear from the start. You'd think being a vamp with guaranteed gorgeousness for eternity would be enough, but no, she wanted to be able to do magic, too.

I dropped the attitude and met Burton's gaze. He was the only one besides Ava and Gran that I let see me with my guard down and all my awkward vulnerability. I had to fix it. "What will happen to Grace? Surely they'll realize it's a mistake." If not, she couldn't pay the price for my indiscretion.

His shoulders lifted slightly. "As far as I know, this hasn't happened before. No one mixes magic with hockey. I'm not sure how the SHL will retaliate."

❧ 4 ❧

"Retaliate?" My stomach rolled at the thought. "Don't they do an investigation first?"

The volume on the TV increased as someone changed the station back to the news. Sully's face filled the television screen as he denied ever meeting Grace and that magic had any role his recent hockey hot streak. The tense line of his jaw portrayed outrage at the accusation.

My phone vibrated in my pocket. "It's Ava." Relief flooded through my tense limbs. She'd know what to do. Burton nodded as if the situation was resolved, reminding me how much I relied on my sister. "Ava?"

"This is ludicrous. Blame the witch." The noise of surrounding traffic cut into Ava's raised voice. "Ridiculous! Grace is the least likely witch to cast an unauthorized spell. I'll hit them with the threat of a discrimination suit so fast their head will spin. I'm on my way there now."

"Ava! I'm responsible for—"

"Don't worry about it. I know you're busy and probably short staffed without Grace. I'll take care of it. I'll have this mistake fixed before the end of your shift."

She concluded the call with a click. There was a mistake all right, but I'd made it. I'd been about to tell Ava ... but perhaps she could rectify this. Working for Just My Type as a Magic Manager, Ava was a witch to be reckoned with. Luckily, she was currently in Florida to clear up another case of magical mayhem.

I replaced the phone in my pocket and met Burton's accusatory stare. He didn't have to say anything for me to know exactly what he was thinking. "I was about to tell her."

He raised one brow a minuscule amount, again.

"Really, I was." I surveyed the rapidly filling club. Most eyes were fixed on the screen, which featured Sully's image. I paused. Proving Sully's innocence from spelling would exonerate the witch, as well.

The camera panned back to the front of the arena to capture the words of the reporter. The bum was still slumped on the corner. I hoped Joe didn't decide to watch the news for once in his life. "Do you think it would've been too much to ask Ava to grab Joe's hat off that bum on her way into the arena?"

Burton held his silent, accusatory stare.

"Don't worry. If Ava doesn't prove Grace's innocence, I will." I chose not to clarify that taking care of it might not mean throwing myself at the mercy of the SHL. I'd have to figure out a way to fix this mess on my own because unlike Grace; I didn't have a pristine spelling record. One glance at the black streak in my hair would be enough to place judgment.

Thank goodness Joe wasn't the type to fix and tell, or else they'd have evidence to build a case of unscrupulous spelling against me. I ran my hand over the ebony strand. I could only hope he didn't hold a grudge about the hat.

THE CROWD PARTED AS THE THREE HOCKEY PLAYERS entered the club. The pack of gorgeous, muscled men couldn't have been ignored. Their smiles lit the room with an air of jubilation. Most likely resulting from the team's win, which the men at the bar had cheered for as it aired on TV earlier tonight.

Our tables encouraged self-seating, although that didn't stop Samantha from trying to escort the players to her table. I stumbled as she pushed me out of the way, and another waitress tried to intercept. I recognized the player a head taller than the rest with dark, longer-than-fashionable hair despite the lack of his trademark number sixty-nine. Mr. Sexy himself. Sully.

While the waitresses squared off to lay claim to the players' seating arrangements, the hockey players chose to seat themselves. Unfortunately, it wasn't at either of their tables. It was one of mine.

As Burton walked to the waitresses with a purposeful stride, they separated. He didn't have to say much; his expression and a few key gestures had them scurrying. But not before they joined forces to identify their newfound enemy—me.

I sighed. Like I wanted the players in my section. Although, this could've been my chance to determine if I'd accidentally spelled Sully and see if I could find out anything to help clear Grace.

After a pointed look from Burton, I headed toward them.

I gave the players my most bewitching smile. My gaze kept straying to Sully. I glanced away when it seemed my attention was making him squirm. "Hello, boys. What can I get you?"

Sully was the first to speak up. "A club soda with lime, please."

His blond crew-cut buddy scowled. "Seriously, Sully? This is the start of your notorious career as a star player, and you want club soda?"

"We're in season," Sully said, and then averted his gaze after his feeble excuse.

"We don't have a game tomorrow, and one drink isn't going to kill you. Come on, one shot to toast another hat trick?" The peer-pressuring player, who was most likely a were, judging by the long brown unruly curls and huge physique, patted Sully on the shoulder as the other guy yelled in agreement.

"Fine. One shot. But that's all." Sully didn't look happy about veering from his regime, but the corner of his lip had pulled up at the compliment. He looked to me expectantly.

"What kind of shot?" I smiled.

Sully faltered and averted his gaze. "Umm ..." His quick smile said he had found a solution. "How about you recommend something?"

His smile caught me by surprise, and I lost my usual superficial retort. "Umm ..." I parroted Sully's initial response as I got lost in his dark eyes while an idea formed.

"I'll make you something special. We can call it, the hat trick." This might've been the answer to my potential dilemma. In addition to getting Sully out of the situation with his friends, I could charm his drink to counteract any spell I may have inadvertently cast.

The guys cheered. "That's awesome! You're getting your own drink, Sully."

"That's something for a guy who rarely drinks— during the season," he said.

I read his pointed look loud and clear. He didn't want something strong.

"Gotcha. Wanna start with that, boys?" With their approval, I returned to the bar, mulling over what to put in the drink. I might have few talents, but I was becoming Vlad's best witch mixologist— whether he realized that yet or not. I mean, I was his only witch mixologist, and on probation, but still. Perhaps one day I could stay behind the bar instead of delivering drinks.

As I raised my hand over Sully's drink, preparing to counteract anything I may have inadvertently cast the other night, I felt a presence behind me. He'd arrived soundlessly, but I had no doubt who it was.

"Do you think that's a good idea?" Burton's voice carried over my shoulder.

I lowered my hand. I'd have to think of another way to deal with Sully. Burton would be watching me all night while I waited on the players. Plus, as expected, the stink eyes of the waitresses weren't far behind. They were looking for an opening to yank the table from me. I didn't respond to Burton. There was no need to. We both knew it wasn't a good idea. Most of the things I did weren't.

I returned to the table with my head held high despite the weight of Samantha's glare. The players were going to love this shot. Since a hat trick meant three goals, I used three ingredients, but their identity would remain a secret.

"Ready to try out the hat trick, fellas? A mix of slashing, scoring, and spectacular." I included each player in my sweeping gaze. "Let me know what you think."

Sully appeared as uncomfortable with the attention as a vamp in a garlic-scented shawl and hesitated as he lifted the glass. He cast a glance at me, and I rested a hand on his shoulder. "Don't worry. I made it just how you like it." A wink provided him with the reassurance to down his shot made of mostly sparkling water.

The beat of my favorite song echoed across the dance floor. When I glanced to Jamming Geno in the DJ Booth, he nodded, with a meaningful gaze at my hand resting on Sully's shoulder. He knew I couldn't resist this song. It was how he filled the dance floor— a task I embraced. No one wanted to be first on the floor. No one ... except me.

"Would you like to dance?" If Sully hadn't finished his shot, he might've choked on it at the suggestion.

"Dance? I can't dance."

"Everyone can dance." Not everyone was any good at it, but dancing was about having fun. "Besides, aren't you naturally graceful? I've seen you on the ice. Toss in a few of those moves."

Jamming Geno's stare boring into my back confirmed his impatience with the deserted dance floor. The players chanted Sully's name, encouraging him to join me. He stood with reluctance. I grasped his hand and tugged him behind me. The nearby tables cheered, and Jamming Geno added a few scratches to the mix.

I turned to face Sully, sashaying my hips as I backed toward the dance floor. I loved dancing, but apparently Sully didn't. Having a celebrity partner increased the pressure on me. I hadn't considered how much focus would follow him. The flush rising along his neck was visible despite his golden skin tone.

"I can't do this. I told you. I don't dance. I'm going to look like an idiot," he said and stepped away.

I grabbed his hand. He looked at it and frowned, as if preparing to protest. "No," I said. "You won't." I shimmied to the beat and then stood on my toes to yell over the music, and for a whiff of his musky masculine scent. "Stand still. I'll let you know when to move."

He allowed me to lead him. The huge disco ball Geno insisted Vlad install sent tiny sparkles of light over everything. When Sully reached the center of the dance floor, I gestured for him to stop. The lights washed over his chiseled features, making me lose my step and suck in a breath. He looked like an angel.

No. Angels hadn't been around for years now, and certainly not in Bayo, Florida. At least that was what Gran had told me. With all manner of paranormals coming into the club, I'd never met an angel, so I believed her. It must have been the reflection from the disco ball giving Sully extra brilliance. I blinked a few times to regain my focus. I'd heard angels could have that affect—but so did sexy hockey dudes.

As the music filled me, my blood pounded along with the beat. I sashayed around him. His gaze followed me while he remained frozen. I moved toward and away from him and led him as needed, making it seem as though together we had created an elaborate dance.

Sully's shoulders lowered as he relaxed. He was the only thing filling my gaze, as his eyes locked with mine. I was supposed to be finding out if he was spelled, or if he knew anything about Grace, but my only thought was how easily I could drown in his eyes. When the song ended and another blared on in its place, I paused to catch my breath.

"Thanks," he said with a smile tugging at the corner of his lip.

I swallowed the words I wanted to say and acted as if the dance hadn't affected me. Although I was fearful that my body language was broadcasting my thoughts as if I'd put them on the arena jumbotron.

He dipped his head while his eyes sought mine. I rose on my toes to meet his tentative kiss. As we separated, someone jostled me from behind. I turned to meet Samantha's glare. "Table six needs to order."

"I guess I better get back to work so you can celebrate with your friends," I said. An irrational part of me that didn't value my job, or wasn't worried about getting shanked by a vengeful vamp, wanted him to insist that I stay. But he didn't.

I returned to the bar to retrieve my tray. Burton shook his head when I met his unblinking stare. "What? Geno wanted the dance floor filled. It's full. Plus, you know once people start dancing, they get thirsty and then buy more drinks. That makes Vlad happy, and it should make you happy because you can make more tips."

Burton usually lacked the ability to charm our customers into lingering and buying extra drinks. A few complained that he scared the bats out of their belfries. "You'd make more if you smiled occasionally and acted a tiny bit friendly," I said.

He bared his teeth in a half-hearted attempt at a smile. The image was more frightening than a jack-o-lantern on Halloween night.

I drew back. "On second thought, don't bother."

People were milling around the players, vying for autographs and photographs. What if Sully, or one of the players, had made up the accusation of a spell for the attention it was giving the team? It certainly had put them in the spotlight.

If only I could've figured out how to make sure I hadn't spelled Sully. It wasn't like I could've asked if he happened to notice the tingle of a spell right before his first goal at the end of the second period. Plus, I doubt he'd be able to get Joe's hat back. My karma really must be in the crapper.

Surely, by now, Ava would have everything righted with Grace. My sister was more relentless than a were seeking his mate when she latched onto something. No use worrying about spilled nacho cheese spells before it was necessary. But maybe there was something else I could do if Ava hadn't freed Grace yet.

5

"I've been bartending for five years, sir," I said. I needed this temporary job to gain access into the arena. Grace had to have been somewhere here. Ava hadn't yet cleared her of this mess—and it was *my* mess. I should at least try to fix it myself and hopefully not make things worse. Perhaps I could find out if Sully was to blame for any of this.

The meek attitude I struggled to project fit me like a shirt two sizes too small, but desperate times called for desperate measures. I'd barely slept all night waiting to hear back from Ava. It was time to act. I hadn't told anyone of my plan, not even Jasper; most likely, he'd tell me to wait until Ava resolved everything.

After tiring of staring at the plastic name badge of the hiring manager named Jim, I studied the purple and gold polish adorning my fingers, which lay inter-twined on my lap. Due to the conflict-of-interest clause, I couldn't list Night Moves on my resumé if I wanted to keep my job. Bartending within a twenty-mile radius was cause for immediate termination.

My head ached from the painfully tight braid concealing the black streak. When the investigation was announced, many of the witches who worked for the arena were outraged at the accusation against Grace and had quit. Others had remained, and their defiant actions challenged management's patience. Both situations left them with a need for temporary help until this was resolved.

Jim lifted my resumé between his fingers and sighed. He raked his gaze over me, looking none too pleased with what he saw. Which was probably a docile witch who'd flee at the first drunken insult. Hopefully he wouldn't check my fake references. Calling the random numbers I'd listed would connect Jim to a confused fast food worker wondering why someone was requesting a reference instead of a meal. But I knew the arena was desperate for help and probably anxious to ensure they wouldn't get hit with a witch discrimination suit since Ava had started stirring that pot.

The door swung open.

A thin, frazzled vamp startled us both as he disregarded containing his speed and rushed the desk. "Jim! We're down three more bartenders. After the last news segment with that blonde ranting about discrimination and how no witch with any integrity would lower themselves to work for us, the last of the witches quit on the spot."

Jim's eyes met mine. I tilted my head, permitting a little confidence to leak into my stare. The vampire quieted and followed Jim's stare, noticing me for the first time. His delicate nose twitched, no doubt identifying the light scent of magic most vampires detected on a witch.

"How soon can you start?" Jim said.

"Let's discuss my wages." I smiled.

❧

Being the lone female witch tossed in with a mostly male supernatural cesspool at the arena wasn't nearly as fun as it sounded. They didn't need to verbalize their distrust of a witch willing to work at the arena in light of the current events. Not when every one of them was eyeing me warily.

I'd thought the arena was big when I came for the hockey game and the occasional concert before, but I'd never been in all the nooks and crannies. It was like a hive buzzing with activity. Although, half the worker bees had now fled from the nest. This left no one to orient me other than the unfortunate vamp who happened upon me when Jim hired me.

Lee had lingered outside the women's locker room as I located my employee locker and changed into my uniform. His strained smile had his incisors cutting into his lip. His restraint made him appear as if his face was frozen in an expression of uncomfortable constipation. But for now, he had to tolerate me. His impatience—and their lack of staff—had him hustling off to address some other crisis before I finished.

That, and I ticked him off when I asked him if Lee was short for LeStat on our walk to the locker room. The way his brows pinched, and his vehement denial, confirmed it was. The witch walkout didn't help to endear him to witches. Who knew a tiny nacho cheese spell could start so much trouble?

I peeked out of the locker room and confirmed the coast was clear. I mean, *really* clear. It wasn't just Lee that was gone—the long hallways stretched empty as far as I could see.

I grimaced.

I had a hard enough time trying to blend in, but it was going to be particularly challenging if I was the only person around. There was no game today, and Lee suggested that I get used to the layout to prepare for the next game tomorrow. That would be my excuse if I ran into anyone while I was poking around.

The vendors working the aisles toting tubs of booze and snacks up and down endless flights of stairs were mainly male vamps. The stairs didn't wear them out, plus they were lithe and lightning fast. The weres' strength made it easy for them to carry stuff, but they usually worked the halls since their bulk occluded the view of the game and blocked the walk-way. I'd be working at one of the bars.

Bartending would be helpful. If I was behind a bar somewhere, then I wouldn't have as much risk of running into a witch who would report me to the ones who had walked out. I was an outcast on both sides, no matter how you looked at it, but I needed to be here to find Grace. I'd figure out what to do next once I did.

I scanned the doorways, wincing as my heels clacked noisily against the tile floor and wishing I'd brought sensible shoes. The heels looked absurd with my twill pants and cotton shirt. It made me appear like a kid playing dress-up. But I didn't think I'd be starting the job the moment I walked in. I should've pressed for a higher pay rate.

The hall loomed long and empty. Generally, I lived by the seat of my pants, but it looked like I needed a plan to determine which objective to work toward first.

I held up my hand as I contemplated my options and ticked off each gold and purple colored fingernail.

Figure out where Grace was and break her the heck out of here—it wasn't like the SHL had any right to keep her imprisoned.

Track down Sully and determine if I'd spelled him and make that right ... somehow.

Stop at the corner to retrieve Joe's coveted, and now probably cruddy, hat from the bum.

The hat seemed like the easiest task to tackle first. I could pop outside, find the bum, coerce him with something to get the darn hat back, and be able to cross one item of my to-do list.

I pushed the side door open a crack—enough to detect the underlying stench of angry magic brewing. Witches lined the front of the arena, daring anyone to cross the line to work.

Forget that plan. No wonder I was hired immediately. I'd never make it back in if I left now. Getting out would be a different story. I could only hope they had a back door somewhere in this maze. I let the door close softly to avoid detection.

Perhaps I should move to Plan B: Find Grace and bust her out of wherever they were holding her in the arena before anyone was the wiser. I could focus on Sully and determine whether I needed to fix a magical mess later. If all the fuss about how quickly he'd risen to hockey superstar status had died down, it would be easier to approach him. Then I could get a better idea if I'd spelled him while cleaning up the nacho mess.

I nodded at the approaching were who was balancing a big box of merchandise and then averted my gaze under his heavy stare. No need to call unnecessary attention to myself by standing here in indecision. I started down the hall with a confident stride as if I knew my destination.

My heel twisted on the tile, and I fell into the were as he passed, jostling the box from his hands. "I'm so sorry!"

So much for being discreet.

The box slid across the floor and came to a stop on its side, and a jumble of hats spilled out. A quick glance confirmed they looked nothing like Joe's coveted hat. *Cauldrons!* There wouldn't be an easy fix to replace his blasted hat.

I leaned forward for a closer inspection and sighed. The focus on Sully was gaining momentum. The number sixty-nine was embroidered across the bills with the words, *Hat Trick 69.*

The were scowled and scooped up the hats.

"Thanks for the help, *witch*. I suppose you expect special treatment, or you'll cry discrimination, huh?"

He stalked away before I could sputter a reply.

I frowned and cocked a hip, prepared to yell a snarky retort at his retreating ginormous shoulders until the cotton fabric of my pants bunching under my tense fist reminded me that I was an employee here now.

I sighed, realizing I probably did appear lazy staring at the mess I created instead of offering to help while he picked up the hats.

Apparently, the employees thought I expected to be pampered.

If I went outside, the witches on strike might hex me into the next decade for working here.

My shoulders fell in defeat at what felt like a situation where I would lose either way. *Whatever.* Best get started. So far, my coworkers were colder than the ice filling the rink.

I picked up my pace down the hall, stopping to try, and fail, to open each door I passed. Grace had to have been here somewhere.

Each knob I jiggled and each door I pushed against held strong. They were all locked. All I was getting for my efforts was a sore shoulder—until I shoved the next door. My frustration had me exerting extra momentum since I expected it to be locked.

It wasn't.

It swung inward, taking me with it.

I stumbled in the room, my heels skidding across damp tile as I flailed my arms until I stopped short of taking a nosedive to the floor.

I surveyed the area. The air hung heavy with a damp mist.

I tensed.

Someone was in here with me.

I could sense them.

That, or it could've been the shadow the low lighting cast against the tile wall.

The mist caressed a shadowy form. As the fog parted, I glimpsed broad, defined shoulders sprinkled with droplets of water from the shower.

Broken broomstick! I should've turned and skedaddled out faster than a spelled spider to avoid providing an awkward explanation justifying that I wasn't a voyeur in the men's locker room.

I took a slow step back, trying to escape before he either smelled me or heard me— depending upon whether he was vamp or were. His build was too perfect to be merely mortal.

As the mist cleared my gaze—which had been focusing on his firm butt—I froze, realizing he was none of the above when I noticed the wings emerging from his back.

Holy mother of molten chocolate.

The skin rippled on his back. I gasped as it seemed to melt away, and the first signs of feathered wings were revealed. They were still folded and tucked along his back, but they began to stretch and lengthen to below his waist.

Those weren't small, delicate wings of the Fae, nor like anything I'd ever seen on a shifter. I'd never met an angel, but that sure as heck looked like what he was.

I'd heard angels were basically extinct on earth. No wonder he was showering alone. Did anyone realize they had an angel on the team? The padding would conceal his wings if he wanted to keep his true origins secret.

His wings lifted and opened slightly.

They fluttered, and a few droplets of water fell.

I stared, wondering how those immense appendages could close so compactly on his back. It was almost like magic.

After a few shakes, he opened them until they were fully extended and brushed the surrounding walls.

My breath caught.

They were beautiful.

Tiny feathers, layered row upon row. I longed to touch them to discover their texture. Maybe I could get a little closer. Who knew if I'd have an opportunity to see angel wings up close again?

I stretched my arm out and took a step. I still wasn't close enough.

His shoulders tensed, and he snapped his head up.

Uh oh. I dropped my arm to my side.

Those glorious wings folded so fast that they created a gust of wind and lifted my hair with their retreat. Within seconds, the wings molded into his back and blended in with his skin until they were invisible to the naked eye.

Fiddlesticks!

I racked my brain for a feasible explanation as to why I was in the men's shower room and why I was standing there gawking like a peeping Tilly instead of announcing my presence or retreating. Nothing convincing came to mind.

Too late.

He turned to face me.

6

No wonder he'd chosen this time of day to hide out in the shower room. Besides wanting the privacy to clean his wings, he probably wasn't getting much peace since his face was plastered all over the news. His brows rose and lowered, and then settled into an expression of confusion.

Sully.

Despite his questioning stare, my tongue remained paralyzed and the capability to speak eluded me.

"Who are you, and why are you in the men's locker room?" He asked with a narrowed gaze.

Unfortunately, I didn't have a plausible lie on the tip of my tongue, so I went with the truth. Not the whole truth about how I was ogling him, how I may have cast a spell on him, and how I was the same cocktail waitress that had shaken my money maker all over him.

I cringed.

I didn't know much about angels, but I couldn't imagine they thought much of brazen witches.

His ran a hand along his ribcage and then let it fall as if ensuring his wings were stashed.

"I'm new here, and I'm lost." I blinked as my eyes watered from the steam. Hopefully he'd think the perspiration beading on my face was from the heat of the shower room and not because my female hormones were going into overdrive.

His eyes strayed to my arena shirt and then to my hands. I tried to keep them dangling in front of me instead of instinctively bracing them on my hips to square off like he was one of the drunks from the club.

The club!

Moonlighting and alibis! I needed to get to the club in time for my shift, or I'd have more explaining to do today.

His defensive posture relaxed. Apparently deciding a damp, droopy, knit-shirt wearing woman wasn't a threat. "Oh. I thought you were another reporter."

"Is that why you're in here alone?" I wanted to

clarify that there weren't any other half-naked men lurking. As appealing as that scenario sounded, I didn't want to start interrogating Sully about whether he'd been spelled. Then, if so, determine how to remove it if another dude was going to stroll out of the mist and distract me with his... uh, hockey stick.

"It's a shower room." He stated the obvious while looking at me with interest, as if still trying to establish my motive.

Unfortunately, I could only assume he'd concluded that I was a fan stalking him. I didn't want to set a personal record in getting fired within the first few hours of a new job. That feat usually took me at least a day.

"I know that, butt-wonker." I winced when the sarcasm rolled off the tongue, one which my mother often insisted was barbed. Nerves usually resulted in inappropriate laughter or sarcastic responses. These were the times when I wished I had more control over my loose lips.

"Did you just call me—"

I hurried to rectify my rude response. "I wanted to see if there was anyone else I owed an apology to for barging in here."

That sounded lame even to my own ears.

Sully's expression didn't appear as if he'd heard my

pitiful excuse. It was difficult to discern if he was amused or irritated. "Is that even a word?"

Exasperation won over my feeble attempts at deceit. "I didn't call you a butt-wonker."

"So, you do think it's a word? And obviously you did call me that, or you wouldn't remember what you said." His frown couldn't even begin to tarnish all his angelic glory. "Wait a minute. I know you."

"No, I—" The thud of the outer shower door cut off whatever stupid thing I was about to say. I needed to take a page from Ava's book of manners and accept not having the last word. Goddess knows she had to get accustomed to that early on, growing up with me.

"What in Dracula's tomb are you doing in the men's shower room?" Lee's outrage had his voice sounding like a squeak. His gaze narrowed on me, but not before I saw it stray over to Sully. His momentary loss of professional demeanor validated that I wouldn't be able to coerce him with my feminine wiles. Not with a smorgasbord of delectable dudes to catch his wandering eye.

"I got lost, butt—" My second attempt at the semi-lie was less successful than the first, and my deliberate avoidance of the word butt-wonker made the fib more obvious.

Lee rolled his eyes, which repeatedly kept darting

over to take in Sully. He lingered on every ounce of exposed flesh, before returning to me. Once he focused on me, his gaze narrowed.

Lee's lip pulled up in a slight smirk. "Stop harassing the players. If you had taken a moment to review your orientation manual, you'd have realized that's rule number one. If the boss wasn't so dire for staff, you'd already be out the door. Let's leave Mr. Sexton to his shower."

He took a step toward Sully and shifted his attention away from me. His expression softened and with the eagerness of a puppy—or more like a bloodhound—and he said, "Unless you require anything from me, Mr. Ssssexton?"

He added a come-hither look which might've been attractive if it was on anyone else. It seemed more like he was struggling not to pass gas.

The look appeared wasted on Sully. He raised a brow. "No thanks, I'm fine. Besides, she wasn't harassing me."

I started at Sully's unexpected defense. A stranger having my back wasn't usual.

Lee shuddered. Probably a result of the fantasy bubble that had formed in his porcelain noggin bursting. "Let's go witch—err, Marissa."

I SLID ONTO A WOBBLY STOOL TO GATHER MY energy to face the growing crowd at Night Moves. Staking out the arena had left me with little time to prepare for work, and the looks I was getting confirmed that a little more time, and maybe some makeover magic potion, might've been beneficial.

The large mirror surrounding the bar reflected my droopy, lackluster locks that only emphasized the black streak. I had tried twisting my mane into a jumbled hairstyle to conceal the blatant beacon of shame better. Granted, most of the regulars had seen the humiliating streak before. They either made a rude comment about it, raised a brow, or relaxed into a comfortable position of superiority, but I still didn't like to display it.

The arena shift had been exhausting but uneventful. While wandering around in Lee's nonexistent shadow, I repeated my made-up mantra to remind myself why I was trying to keep up with a vexed vamp and to avoid contemplating Sully's secret angel status. *"Free Grace, fix Sully, find hat."*

Lee made me carry the orientation manual with me as we sprinted through the arena. Well, he sprinted with his freakish vamp speed while I plodded behind. He claimed the massive book was a necessary reference as he reiterated the rules, but I thought he was punishing me for the incident with

Sully. The darn book felt like it weighed a metric ton since pages had been added to it ongoing for the last hundred years.

I asked Lee why in the *golden goddess* they didn't use a magic minimizer to condense the information. This only led to a lengthy lecture about how using any magic in the arena was forbidden. Like he had to remind me. I wouldn't be in this situation if I'd not learned that lesson the hard way.

Lee had prevented me from finding out anything about Grace or determining if Sully had been spelled. Perhaps being an angel made him glide across the ice like that, and not magic. But I would've thought some of that skill would've shown up before I did.

I lifted a foot, wincing as I rubbed it. "He didn't even make an effort to slow his vamp warp speed," I muttered to myself. These heels were okay for walking, but not for flights upon flights of stairs. I'd be sure to bring comfortable shoes next time.

The most interesting thing was what I hadn't learned, and that was anything about the SHL. As much as I had pressed Lee, I couldn't find out anything about who was behind Grace's detainment. Now discovering that the player in the center of this whole fiasco was an angel... Well, that made no sense. Could angels be spelled?

I frowned and wondered if there was a rule

against angels in hockey. If I ever took the time to flip through the massive book that made my neck and shoulders ache, I might find out.

Sully had to know I saw his wings, yet he didn't say anything about them. How did he know I wouldn't blab? His angel status had to have been a secret, or it would've been public knowledge to the paranormal community by now since he was a star player. If witches couldn't use magic in the game, what did that mean for angels? Was he trying to deflect suspicion about his abilities by blaming magic? There had to be more to this story. If only I had the chance to talk this through with Gran or Ava, or even Jasper.

Luckily my arena shift had been cut short since I made the excuse of having another obligation. It wasn't like I expected to start working the moment I entered the arena. I also didn't reveal that the obligation was my other job. Nor did I mention my biggest concern about one of the job requirements—being able to ice skate. I was sure I could with the help of a smooth skating spell, but unfortunately, that wasn't an option.

How could I learn how to skate by tomorrow? Maybe they could relax the requirements since they were desperate for employees. But Lee seemed to harbor quite a dislike for me, and I'd bet he wouldn't make an exception no matter how hard up for staff they were.

What was the big deal about skating, anyway? It wasn't like I was one of the Ice Angels who had to go out between plays. The name for the team's cheerleaders was kind of ironic, considering that they had an absolute, true-to-goodness angel on the team.

I rubbed at my neck, trying to find the energy to start my table rounds. But I couldn't help thinking how barbaric the whole hockey thing was. I was sure it went back to the SHL—whoever those mysterious rule makers were—since they made the ridiculous requirements. They acted as if magic didn't exist. What was the point of living as a supernatural being if you couldn't use your abilities?

It wasn't like they could make the vamps walk at a normal speed. Believe me, I would've liked to find a way to slow Lee's narrow little behind down as I trailed him up and down a bazillion sets of steps.

And they never considered forbidding the weres from using their superhuman strength.

Nope.

The only ones who were restricted in using their abilities were witches. Maybe Ava was right and something needed to be said to support the witches. I could only wish she would decide to say it when I wasn't directly involved.

Speak of the devil—or I should say, the witch.

Ava marched into the club, pivoting her head to scan the room. It wouldn't be long before her gaze found me. I didn't refer to her as Eagle-Eyed-Ava for nothing.

"Hi, Sis." I smiled weakly, and Ava's brows furrowed in concern; she appeared to mistake my exhaustion for distress.

She laid a hand on my shoulder. "Don't worry. We'll have Grace out of there in no time."

Guilt washed over me. Here I was wallowing in pity about flights of stairs and worrying about learning to ice skate when my friend was enduring goddess knows what, and it was my fault. "I know. We will."

I knew that when Ava said *we* in this situation she was only being kind by including me in the rescue party. But this time, I was going to help. I'd have done so even if Grace's situation wasn't my fault.

"What can angels do?" I blurted the question in my usual manner of digressing from the topic when I didn't want Ava to detect my underlying lies. Plus, besides Gran, she knew more stuff than any witch I knew. If anyone had answers, it was Ava.

Ava raised a perfectly plucked brow. "Why? Have you taken to praying for Grace? There's more that we can do before we rely on an angel's help."

"No, not for Grace. I mean, sure, if it would help. But I was more curious for me." I shrugged.

"Sis, I love you, but I think you've got more devil in you than angel most days." She patted me on the shoulder.

I rolled my eyes. Either she didn't want to take the time to explain it to me, or she didn't know. Not that I had any time now either, with Burton giving me *the* pointed look. The one I deciphered as his signal to get my butt moving cause the boss was on his way.

Burton's hearing was supersonic. I didn't know if it was because of his intense focus on everything that enabled him to pick up any sound, or because he was a demon, but he was never wrong.

I hopped off the stool to get this shift going. I had to go back to the arena tomorrow. Perhaps between now and then I'd squeeze in learning how to ice skate. Or at least figure out a way to keep Lee off my back.

7

"**W**here have you been?" Jasper's whiskers tickled my face.

I rolled to the side, but he climbed over my hip and crouched down in my face. "You've barely been home for days, and I have to read it in the *Willow Words* that Grace has been arrested."

The *Willow Words* was part of the reason I'd been avoiding the condo. Fran Stokes, who compiled the witches' retirement condo newsletter, was bound to be staking me out for the scoop. "You would've read a lot more, if I had been around more."

Fran would embellish anything I said to make it into a story. These retirees acted as if they had nothing to lose, which meant Fran had no qualms about stretching, bending, and expanding upon the truth to get a story. With Gran away on her cruise, I had lost my buffer, and the witches living in the retirement condo descended upon me. I'd hoped having Ava here to visit would deter their attention, but my sister wasn't here much, either.

"You can't leave me home alone," Jasper said with a whine.

"You aren't alone. You have Mulder and Savvy." I flopped onto my back, realizing it was fruitless to try to sleep.

Jasper's almond-shaped eyes widened. "You're kidding, right? Besides Mulder being his usual annoying slobbery self, your sister's cat is just ... snooty."

I rolled my eyes. Savvy wasn't snooty. Jasper was just intimidated and maybe a little infatuated with the feline. I sat up. "I'm trying to help Grace."

Jasper walked across the comforter with his tail held high. "You mean help Grace out of the mess you created?"

I stood and went to the closet. "I don't have time for your reprimands, and besides, I get enough lectures from Ava. I have to get ready to go to the arena."

He sprang onto the chair beside my tote bag. "I'm ready to go."

My uniform looked a little worse for wear since I'd left it crammed in my bag in my rush to change for Night Moves, but it would have to do. Hopefully this would be my last day working there. "You're not going."

"Admit it. You need me," Jasper hissed.

"Give me one reason why I need you at the arena that is not an excuse to avoid Mulder and Savvy?"

"One reason? I can give you plenty. I'm the one who has been the key factor in your ability to solve a murder and other crimes, and even discover which one of the witches in the community was going through our mail. Plus, I don't need permission to sneak around the arena. Once I'm in, I'm in. I can find Grace, or at least find out who's behind this way faster than you can. I already have a list of suspects," Jasper said with a smile.

"So do I," I said. "Sully, because it distracts from his secret about being an angel and it gave the team instant fame. Gloria, because... Well, she's earned that coal-black hair somehow. Samantha, because that vamp would love to throw a witch under the bus, and getting Grace fired would mean more tips for her since Grace is a customer favorite." I couldn't blame the customers; Grace was the nicest person I knew.

I hopped on one foot as I shoved a leg into my pants. "And maybe Burton, because he'd love to increase others' interest in hockey since he loves it so much. He's said as much since the games aren't always televised. It's hard to maintain interest in a frigid sport in a sweltering state. Not to mention that he's a demon." I hated to once again toss Burton into the list of suspects, but he should've been used to suspicion by now.

Jasper paused from cleaning his paw to say, "I hate to burst your bubble, but the only ones that would have any power to hold Grace at the arena would be Burton or Sully."

The furball had a point. "How do you know anything about this when you've never even left the condo?"

"I have ears, and your sister has been here a few times making calls. She might not understand what I have to say, but I can understand her. Besides, you know what they say: Curiosity filled the cat."

That wasn't how the saying went, but correcting him would've been a waste of my time. "But I can't get you into the hockey arena."

Jasper crawled into my tote bag and poked his head out. "You can, and you will."

EVEN THOUGH ABOUT EVERYONE WHO WORKED AT the arena was prejudiced against witches, some still appreciated the benefits of a potion. At least Zeke the security guard did. Most likely he'd never admit to allowing me in early, or the suspicion that I had a cat under my coat, in exchange for a desirability potion.

I slipped in one of the arena's side doors so I could snoop around before my shift. And so my face wouldn't be plastered on television if the news crew lining the outside of the arena noted my presence. If Ava discovered I was working here, her wrath might've been worse than the witches picketing outside. Plus, I needed to get on the ice to practice since there was the whole learning how to skate without the help of magic thing.

Once inside, I released Jasper to go poking around while I snuck down to the ice. The cool temperatures that were initially a welcoming reprieve from the Florida heat were downright frigid this close to the ice. I scanned the rows upon rows of empty seats and imagined how it must've looked to the players when they saw the eager—or angry—faces, depending on how the game was progressing.

My confidence drained when I arrived at the ice. Lee might have made up the rule about ice skating. I should've at least looked in the orientation manual. If I fell and broke something, the humiliation might've been worse than the pain. I was sure the scrawny vamp enjoyed skating since it was probably the only place in Florida as cold as his heart.

Why would a witch living in Florida—or anywhere for that manner—learn to ice skate? They didn't need to when they could use magic. When I lived in Pennsylvania, I could charm a pair of gliding gear without worrying about breaking my neck. It was frustrating to have to learn to skate without the help of a spell when I had other pressing matters to worry about. But I had to try if I wanted to keep this job to make any progress in finding Grace and who, or what, was behind her detainment.

I tapped a foot on the ice and then withdrew it. The ice felt hard, cold, and unforgiving. Surely just being able to stand and move a little would've been adequate? It wasn't like I was trying out for the Ice Angels. My breath fogged in front of me, and my legs wobbled. I wasn't even on the ice yet.

Grace.

I was doing this for Grace.

Well, it was now or never. Falling on my behind a few times had to be nothing compared to what I was putting her through.

I braced myself on the wall and balanced on the borrowed skates. Who in the world thought putting razor-sharp blades on the bottom of a shoe was a good idea? If I was going to fly, it should've been on a broomstick and not ice skates. Alas, duty called.

I tensed and took a tentative step. The ice propelled me a few feet from the wall. The light breeze lifted my hair from my face and chilled my skin.

I smiled.

This wasn't so bad. Maybe I'd be okay at this. I did have decent balance, after all.

I picked up my pace to glide a little faster. My skates carved a thin path across the ice. I was a natural! What was I worried about?

As the wall approached, I started to turn, but not quickly enough that I'd succeed before the impact. It was then that I realized the true challenge of ice skating—stopping.

How in *green leprechauns* were you supposed to stop without a brake? I lifted my arms to balance and had to use every ounce of self-control not to spell the skates into working like well-oiled machines instead of blades of death. If I cast a spell, it was bound to be picked up on whatever wacky magic radar the SHL was using.

Panic set in as I contemplated my complete lack of control. Wasn't there something about putting your feet together like a tank? Or a truck?

Snowplow.

That was it. But how in the heck did you snowplow?

Still not stopping!

Instead, I went further and further into that place where no witch in her right mind and who couldn't skate worth a darn would want to be—in the center of the ice and heading towards the wall.

Inward. That's what it was, something about how to aim your skates. *I think.* It was only a matter of time before I fell and ended up being found frozen to the ice when the Ice Angels came to warm up before the game. They'd be prancing around doing their fancy moves and using me as a speed bump.

I flailed my arms to try to slow my speed and turned my skates inward in the suggested snowplow stance. Since I wasn't losing speed as quickly as I'd hoped, I angled my feet to push my toes further into the ice.

Forget this. I was gonna use magic to spare my behind from a crash. Better to be charged with using magic than breaking a few bones that I'd have to suffer with until I could get to a healer. Surely there were exceptions to magic use when there wasn't a game? For things like avoiding injury and being frozen in embarrassment?

Before I could wrap my mind around a spell to ensure a safe stop, the blade of my skate gripped the ice, I lost my balance and became airborne. *Rusty caldrons!* I was flying, all right. But not in any way I would've liked.

The impact on the cold, hard ice ignited pain in every limb and knocked the breath from my body. I exhaled with a grunt and slid on my side like some fleshy, spinning sled until I bumped into the wall. I lay facing the empty rink. I mentally assessed my body to determine if any of my parts were injured worse than my pride. Even with all the padding the players wore, I gained a new respect for willingly risking falling repeatedly on the hard surface. They must've been insane.

The ice rink looked bigger from this awkward angle. My cheek stuck to the ice, and one of my gloves lay a few feet away. Thank the goddess Lee wasn't here to witness my humiliation.

"Just great." I frowned when my gaze fell on a figure standing at the entrance to the ice. The shadows made him unrecognizable.

I pushed to a sitting position and squinted, but I still couldn't figure out who it was from this distance. If it was Lee, I'd never hear the end of this and would probably lose my job. Perhaps it was Zeke coming back to check on me, or to see about another potion. Maybe he realized he also needed an attraction spell without me having to suggest it.

As the person approached the edge of the ice, I ruled out Zeke. Despite being cast in shadows, there was no way that was Zeke unless he had lost about fifty pounds, gotten a foot taller, and grown a head of hair. That also ruled out Lee, with his physique rivaling a fourteen-year-old boy.

The shadow man stepped on the ice and glided across with the deft grace of an angel that filled me with envy. The wind rippled through his black wavy hair.

I wanted to talk with Sully, but this certainly wasn't the way I'd envisioned it. Especially when he skated as if he didn't need the wings that were tucked out of sight.

He bent effortlessly and scooped up my glove as he passed it and then slowed to a stop in front of me. He bent and held out a hand. "Are you hurt?"

I shook my head, unwilling to verbalize that my ego was hurt more than anything else. I hesitated, studying his hand. It felt much safer sitting on the ground with the long stretch of ice in front of me. Plus, despite my denial, various places on my body did hurt a little.

He must've seen or detected my apprehension. He wiggled his hand. "Come on, I'll help you. I won't let you fall."

"Are you sure you don't want to join me here?" My

attempt at humor failed as my words sounded more pitiful than sassy. Thoughts of Grace had me swallowing my pride. I clasped his hand and he pulled me to standing. When I bumped against his chest, he steadied me by gently gripping my elbows.

I gazed up. Sully appeared much taller this close. *Dang.* He was more gorgeous than I remembered. I bet he had women falling all over him—but not on the ice. He probably thought I was a complete klutz. "I've not done much ice skating."

I wanted to establish that I was a newbie, so there might've been potential for my improvement.

"Why not?"

It would be easy to start blathering on since I excelled in talking over listening. But so far, I'd barely found out anything to determine what Sully knew about the SHL, or been able to discuss whether or not he was spelled—*and hello?* What the heck was up with the secret angel wings? None were topics I could work into a conversation with someone I barely knew.

The silence grew uncomfortable as I realized I was staring at him while dwelling in my thoughts. The heat of a blush warmed my cheeks. "Why would I? This is Florida." I didn't share that I had absolutely no interest in hockey, or ice skating, when he obviously loved it, but I needed to keep him talking.

"So?" His smile was slow. "There are places to ice skate around here."

I rubbed the back of my head, acting as if I was fluffing my curls while I pressed on the tender spot there. "Why would you want to?" There didn't seem to be many positive benefits to skating. Especially if you could fly with a pair of giant wings tucked in your back, although most cities had strict flying zones.

The shifters could get away with it by changing into an animal form so the mortals didn't complain about an overuse or abundance of magic. I hadn't realized there was another species that might've suffered, because who knew there were still angels amongst us? Not that I'd ever looked, but a hockey rink was one of the last places I'd go to find an angel.

"Because I've always wanted to play hockey. With the streak we've been on, it looks like we might have a chance to win the Cup." His gaze grew wistful.

He could have said the streak he'd created, or rather, I might've created. Instead, he gave credit to the team. I liked that about him. He wasn't nearly as cocky as I expected for a hotshot hockey star and an undercover angel.

Just how important was it to keep his secret under wraps? Important enough to let an innocent witch take the blame? That's what I needed to find out.

8

"Come on. I'll help you." Sully nodded toward the span of ice we faced. "Why were you skating if you hate it?"

"I didn't say I hated it." Although I was certain the scowl frequenting my face while on this frozen floor spoke louder than any words.

His raised brows made me rephrase my comment. "Well, maybe I hate it. Apparently, I have to be able to skate to work here. At least Lee made a point to tell me that's a requirement. It's kind of silly, if you ask me. For all I know, Lee made it up. He probably knows most witches have no need to ever learn to skate because we can use magic."

I studied his reaction. He'd stiffened when I referenced my being a witch, but there were no signs of unease to indicate if he had played a role in Grace's arrest. As an angel, surely he would've had some kind of guilty reaction.

Sully smiled and ran a hand through his hair. "Lee didn't make it up. The rationale is that for someone to promote the joy of the game, they have to appreciate the skill required to skate." He frowned. "How did you get hired if you can't skate?"

"They hired me because they're desperate. Then Lee convinced the boss that there were certain requirements that couldn't be overlooked. Lee needs to see a short skating demonstration, or I can't stay," I said.

I hadn't worried about his comment yesterday because I'd been optimistic that I would've already figured out where Grace was and be gone.

"I'm surprised he wouldn't bend the rules due to the staffing crisis." Sully cupped my elbow to steady me.

"Nope. I asked. Lee said it would set a precedence because previous applicants weren't hired if they didn't meet this essential standard. I'm supposed to review the rest of the rules and responsibilities in that supersized orientation book. No wonder so many vamps work here. It probably takes them a thousand years to read that thing." I snapped my mouth shut and looked to Sully. Did he consider Lee as friend or foe? Here I was complaining about the vengeful vamp, and for all I knew, Lee could've been his best friend. "You won't tell Lee that I can't skate, will you?"

"So, you're going to work here?" He ignored my question as he scrutinized me, brows pulled down in concentration.

I nodded, hoping his positive reference to my position here confirmed he didn't intend to blab to Lee. Also realizing that if I didn't stop standing here like cupid's arrow had smacked me in the behind instead of the ice, my time was going to be up. I needed to figure out how to at least do a minimal amount of skating.

"Oh, wait a minute, you're the shower girl," he said.

"Um, well, I don't think that's my official title. It's something along the lines of bar banshee, or something like that, but... Um, yes. That's me. Although I don't usually barge into men's shower rooms." This was definitely not making the best impression. Time to change the subject to get to some relevant information and get off this ice.

"What are you doing here so early? I didn't think anyone started practice until later today." At least that was what I'd been banking on. I could barely stay upright. If a gaggle of players decided to join us, I'd be out on my keister in more ways than one.

Besides my inability to skate, I wasn't allowed to be on the ice now.

He shrugged and appeared uncomfortable with the question. "I like to practice by myself before everyone else. You know, a little extra effort can go a long way."

I wasn't sure I did. Unless he was referring to spelling and potions. But practicing spelling didn't require the blood, sweat, and tears the players had to put into the game. Spelling only required my complaining, cursing, and a cocktail or two to reduce my frustration when I couldn't get it quite right.

"Wait. I've seen you somewhere else." Sully's comment came across a little hesitant, as recognition dawned in his eyes, as well as a fleeting look of embarrassment. "You're the dancing queen."

"Well, no one has named me queen of anything yet. Maybe a princess, although usually that's said in a sarcastic manner." I barked a laugh. "I'm sure you didn't immediately identify me due to my obvious lack of grace." I gestured to the ice. "But I think most people suffer with that when they're balancing on metal blades on a sheet of ice."

Sully turned to meet my gaze. "I'm surprised that you work here."

"Why? Because I can't skate?"

"No. Well, maybe that, but because you're a

witch."

I stopped so quickly that I fumbled on the ice until Sully caught me before I fell. "What's that supposed to mean?" It was hard to appear defiant when I was close enough to identify the scent of his cologne. Darn witch superior olfactory glands that had me inhaling his musky scent like an all-you-can-eat buffet.

He shrugged. "Nothing. I mean because the rest of the witches quit."

"Oh, that." This might've been my chance to get some insight into what Sully thought happened if I continued to play completely clueless. Was he digging for clues? Or was I looking into this too deeply? "Why did they quit?"

"Really? You must not watch the news. This is getting way bigger than hockey."

"Do you think it's true, then? Do you think you were spelled?" I clutched his arm tighter so I could focus on his response rather than remaining upright.

"No." He answered quickly. His brisk tone made me think he was worried about that—or something. I didn't have to be a mind reader to catch him in a lie. Or it could've been that he'd caught my lie since I'd pretended not to know the information I'd just blurted.

Sully waved off the subject. "Enough about that.

Why don't you let me teach you to skate? You taught me to dance, so the least I can do is return the favor."

I had to find a way to change the subject back. If I had to focus on not falling, it would've been unlikely I'd be able to do much interrogating. "That wasn't teaching you to dance. And I don't think standing here while you skate around me would have the same effect."

"No, you'll be fine. You'll see. Although you can't learn by holding onto me," he said.

Holding Sully seemed like the best idea. "What else would I hold?"

He smiled. "Wait here. I'll be right back."

I watched his retreating form as he glided across the ice with the grace of—well, the grace of what he was—an angel. He ducked into the hallway right off the ice and, true to his word, he hurried right back. Thank the goddess he did, because I was afraid to move without him.

What he returned with was way less appealing.

"What is that?"

He skidded to a stop and tapped the large, over-turned bucket in front of him on the ice. "It's for you to hold onto. It's usually for the kids, but one of these will work fine for you. Unless you prefer that I get one of the walkers?"

Neither clutching a large pickle bucket that had

to have held more pickles than I'd eaten in my lifetime, or a walker more suited to an elderly mortal, seemed like a good idea, but he seemed so pleased with himself to have thought of this that I couldn't refuse. "No. This is ... great. Thanks."

"It will help you get comfortable until you're ready to try it on your own." He glided away, making skating seem way easier than it was.

I skated around a while, bracing myself on the bucket with my butt raised high in the air. It might've been a way to get his attention if I wasn't so worried about face planting again and injuring more than my pride.

"Okay. I'm ready." I wasn't, but I didn't have all day, and using him as a prop was preferable to the bucket. Surely once I got going, it would come easy, right?

"Don't watch your feet. Look at me." He held my hands and skated backward effortlessly, as if he could see the rink without turning around. His smile was boyish and showed how much joy he derived from skating. I would've thought angels were too busy being do-gooders and tallying up other people's wrongdoings to have hobbies.

Once I stopped looking down and let him lead me, I felt like I was flying. I smiled. This was why he enjoyed this so much. The cool air of the rink reminded me of Pennsylvania in late fall or winter. The caress of the breeze felt much nicer than the sweaty sheen I was accustomed to from the Florida heat.

I stumbled a bit. Sully caught me and righted me before I could knock us both over. Although, it would take a lot more than me falling into him to knock over this hulk who was used to getting plowed into by men way bigger than me intent on taking him down.

"Thank you." I gripped his arms a little tighter.

"I'm not going to let you get a broken bone, or you'll never learn to love to skate like I do." He lifted me and spun me around.

A small shriek escaped from my lips until my feet landed in front of his and I was facing away from him. The arena whizzed by. He pulled me back, and I molded against him; we skated as if we were one unit.

If I didn't already know he was an angel, I might've thrown out a silly line about him falling from heaven. The thoughts going through my mind as our bodies moved as one across the ice, however, were certain to ensure the pearly gates would be locked for me.

"Relax and let me lead." His warm breath tickled my ear.

He picked up speed and as he moved his feet, and

mine glided along with his. The wind blew my hair from my face so that it pressed against him, making me worry he couldn't see through my mass of curls.

Maybe he was onto me and planned to propel me through the air once we built up enough speed to crack my head on the ice. I tensed. "Sully, slow down."

"Stop worrying. I have you."

"I wasn't ..." No use lying to an angel. I'd either have to ask forgiveness later or end up blurting out the truth due to the guilt weighing on me. "Okay, I'll try."

That was an honest as I could get. It was hard not to worry about face planting at this speed. I was bound to get much more than a sore butt if I fell this time. I truly was flying.

The sound of the speaker being tested cut through my racing thoughts. We must've been skating longer than I realized. Sully steered us toward the edge of the ice, slowing to a stop so I could step onto the carpet. I panted, trying to catch my breath from the exertion.

"If Lee catches me out here ..." I grimaced, feeling guilt at being preoccupied with Sully and forgetting about my true purpose of being at the arena—Grace. "I'm not supposed to be here yet. My shift starts later today."

He braced his hands on his hips and smiled. He wasn't even winded. "He won't. He never comes down to the ice unless he has to. I'll cover for you, if necessary."

I stopped in the middle of untying my skate. "Why?"

"Why what?"

"Why are you being so nice to me?"

"Why wouldn't I?" He seemed genuinely perplexed.

"Oh," I said. His answer made me realize part of me hoped it was more. That he'd say something about sharing the feelings he stirred within me. Being kind must've been an angel thing. "Never mind. Thanks." I turned to hurry down the hall in an awkward gait on the skates.

"Marissa?"

I paused. He was going to call me back and tell me that he felt something that could've made the ice melt if we let it. I turned. "Yes?"

"Don't forget your gloves." He extended them toward me.

My smile faded. "Sure. Thanks. Don't want to lose those. I'll need them to keep me warm." Because it didn't appear like I was going to have a hunky hockey angel volunteering for the job.

9

Zeke put a finger to his lips in the universal sign of keeping his trap shut. I nodded to let him know I understood and handed him another potion in exchange for him ignoring me as I wandered around the back halls of the arena. He gestured down the hall and made some odd signals that only increased my confusion. I didn't know if he wanted me to go that way or not go that way. He'd never do well in a game of charades.

I finally realized he wanted me to go the other direction. He couldn't leave his post or else he'd risk losing his job. I gestured with a thumbs up and nodded that I'd be fine weaving my way down the maze of corridors. At least that's what I tried to convey. It may have looked more like a semi-seizure, but Zeke nodded regardless.

"Find Joe's hat. Figure out if I accidentally spelled Sully. Find Grace and determine who is behind the SHL." I repeated to focus. I had spent my time letting Sully skate me under his spell rather than making progress on my goals.

Jasper popped his head out from my jacket. Remnants of tortilla chips fell from his fur. "So far your score has been a big fat *nada*. At this rate you'll never get a hat trick," he taunted.

"Very funny. You don't have to remind me." I'd been spending way too much time talking about hockey if Jasper knew what the definition of a hat trick was. "Besides, you didn't find out anything useful while slinking around while I was skating. You spent more time checking out the food stands."

"Like you found out anything about the SHL, or spelling Sully, while you were falling all over him on the ice." Jasper twitched his whiskers. "I told you Grace might be stashed with the fixings for the pulled pork nachos. Since the spell was to cover up nacho cheese, perhaps the punishment is to be covered with nacho cheese? No one would ever think to look there."

I rolled my eyes. "That's the most ridiculous excuse I've ever heard and an unlikely place to hold Grace."

"Well, if you hadn't told me how much you

enjoyed those darn nachos, and ever stopped talking about that nacho cheese spell, then maybe I wouldn't have been tempted," Jasper hissed.

I patted his head for him to tuck back into my jacket. "Get down before someone sees me talking to you. I'm skating on thin ice—literally—with this job already. Plus, I'm beginning to think Grace isn't here. They must've moved her to another facility until they're ready for the SHL trial."

Whatever the heck that was, or where it was. Who knew? Maybe Burton? Probably Ava. I needed to see what she'd found out.

The sound of voices echoing off the concrete walls silenced me. They were still far away, but as a witch, my hearing was much more acute.

I hurried down the hall, trying to be quiet, but I couldn't stop my footsteps from echoing in the empty corridors and from Jasper bouncing against me. He was going to be irate, but who knew what other paranormal entities were lurking? Last time I'd tried this, I discovered an angel.

The doors all looked the same, and most were locked. As far as I could tell, I'd not been in this area of the arena before. As the voices got closer, my desperation to find a hiding place grew.

Finally, one of the doors swung opened and I ducked inside. Hopefully, I hadn't barged into another locker room. I turned and leaned against the door to catch my breath.

The strong smell of dark magic confirmed this wasn't a locker room.

"It stinks in here." Jasper's voice was muffled inside my jacket, so I wasn't sure if he was talking about me or the magic.

I waited a moment, listening intently as my eyes adjusted to the dark. There was a large glass room enclosed inside this room. The tinted glass area quivered, and the illumination inside wavered. I knew this type of spell. "Why would the enclosure be spelled to prevent another witch from entering or exiting it?"

A witch?

What witch would be willing to use a spell against another in the midst of the SHL arena? If she was discovered, she would have to reckon with the SHL and the Witches Counsel for acting against one of our own.

I shivered as the magic in the room weighed on me. If Grace was anywhere, it had to be here.

I crept closer. At first glance, the glass area didn't reveal it to be the prison cell that it was. If it wasn't for the magic forcefield, it would've looked like a living space inside. Almost like a tiny apartment.

The woman's back was to me. She sat motionless

on a couch, staring at a blank television screen, appearing lost in her thoughts. I didn't have to see her face to easily recognize those chestnut locks.

I'd found Grace.

Jasper peeked from my jacket to whisper, "I told you she was here."

"I don't see the nacho stand." My excitement waned as I studied the elaborate fortress erected to keep one lone witch imprisoned. Why such an over-the-top fortress? It was as if someone wanted to flaunt their power, or they had a major self-confidence problem when it came to witches. This was more than discrimination; it was either that the SHL was outright fearful of witches, or an attempt at intimidation. But how in *Glenda's golden wand* was I going to get Grace out of here without anyone noticing?

I assumed Grace had been tucked away in a room and forced to endure boring interrogation about what kind of spell she had used and why. Then getting a slap on the hand and told to not let it happen again. I never expected anything like this.

The guilt weighed heavier than the magic in the room.

I moved cautiously as I scanned for charmed boobytraps or other surprises. It seemed they didn't feel they needed any since the strength of the barrier surrounding the glass enclosure was so strong. The relief at finding Grace flooded over me, and I disregarded stealth to rush across the room.

Grace spun at my rapid approach. Anger filled her normally calm, welcoming features until recognition dawned and her expression morphed into surprise. As I neared the enclosure, the magic radiating from it sent waves of resistance, making the air feel more like thick lava. I leaned forward to press onward, stopping short of the glass when sparks flew from it.

My watery smile only made Grace shake her head. She knew who the responsible party was for her imprisonment—me. I whispered, "I'm sorry. I'm going to get you out of here."

Grace pointed at her ears to indicate she couldn't hear what I said. She was practically an expert at lip reading so, more likely, she didn't want to hear my lame excuses, or she had no faith in my ability to follow through on my promise—or a little of both.

Grace pointed at a contraption on the wall and through a series of elaborate gestures indicated that I needed to do something with that thingamajig to talk with her. The cell must've been soundproof.

I recognized the antique wall phone from the old history shows Ava loved. As a witch born after her time, she had a thirst for knowledge about the past.

I'd inadvertently absorbed some information simply by being a bystander in her life.

Despite the confusing security of the room, I picked up the receiver, hesitating as I contemplated the extent of her anger. Perhaps her current residence preventing her from annihilating me with any manner of spells was a good thing. Maybe she'd work all that out of her system before I freed her.

"Hi." I smiled tentatively as guilt's tentacles squeezed a little tighter. Even though she stood across the room, and we were separated by glass, I knew she could see me.

Grace stood with her arms crossed and feet braced.

I heard the creak of the door. Someone was here. Grace was much better than Zeke at conveying a message with a gesture. I recognized her insistence that I needed to hide. The problem was finding a place in this barren space.

I scanned the room, focusing on the dark corners. A row of old bleacher seating was pushed against one of the walls. Once I reached it, I dropped to my knees and crawled underneath, almost dumping Jasper from my jacket in the process. I was out of sight, but depending upon what type of paranormal creature entered, they might smell me.

The seating happened to conceal a hall leading

out of the room. I glanced to it and then back to Grace. If I got caught, there was no way I could help her. She must've realized that and knew I was her best bet when she mouthed the words, *Get Ava*.

I hated to leave her, but she was right. Ava was her best bet. I hurried down the hall, Jasper bouncing against my chest and muttering complaints as I fled.

❧

I HAD NO LUCK REACHING AVA. I DIDN'T WANT TO leave the arena without Grace because I wasn't sure if I could get back in again without Zeke. His shift would be over soon, so I had to start my own at the arena bar. Each minute felt like an eternity as I tried to figure out how to help Grace.

I glanced at the clock. My shift would be over soon, and then I could leave to bring in the cavalry. For now, the only plan consisted of letting Jasper go to see what he could do. I didn't have a lot of faith after he'd spent so much time inspecting the food stands, but he insisted he could be resourceful. Unfortunately, he was my best bet now.

My excuses about needing to leave early for "lady issues" weren't working with Lee. If I got fired now, then I'd never have a chance to help Grace. Thinking of her sitting in that glass enclosure like some kind of specimen made me furious. The anger churning through me gave me a better understanding of the expression of blood boiling, because mine felt close to the edge. It was raging so much that if I drew out a liter, a vamp could have a steaming cup similar to the temperature of my morning coffee.

Who was behind the SHL that thought they could create their own rules?

I studied the bottles lining the shelves of the arena bar as I paced. It felt weird to be stuck behind the granite barrier counters instead of running all over the floor like I did at Night Moves. I didn't think I'd ever have to pull out those old skills and make cocktails the old-fashioned way instead of charming them. I was bound to be a bit rusty. Luckily, most of the crowd here went for beer and weren't looking for the fancy frou-frou ones like the ladies at the club did.

Once the arena doors opened to permit the herd of fans to enter, I didn't have time to worry about mixing inadequacies. I was run ragged up and down the small space behind the bar trying to keep pace with the customers. Everyone wanted their drinks before they went in to sit for the game. Then they relied on the guys selling beer in the aisles to keep their pallet from parching.

The challenge was maintaining personal space

while racing around behind the bar—and I was failing at it. As the only witch working with a couple of vamps, I didn't stand a chance. They moved with lightning speed, and I repeatedly bumped into them and spilled more than one drink.

"Hey, witch."

It took me a minute to recognize the dude from the club who had wanted to see Burton. Steve. I tensed. He couldn't know about the conflict-of-interest clause from Night Moves, but I'd try not to antagonize him so he didn't mention seeing me here to anyone back at Night Moves. "What can I get you?"

His gazed raked over me and he scowled. "I'd rather have the vamp serve me."

I shrugged and stepped aside. "Sure." Normally I'd have a witty remark ready, but no use provoking him further. I had enough things to worry about without a customer complaint. Geesh, and to think I'd been trying to save his hide. That's what I got for my good deed.

Once the game began, the demand for drinks significantly slowed as most of the people went to their seats. When I had a moment for a breather, I studied the screens displaying the game. It made no more sense to me than it did the night I came with Grace, except now I knew one of the players.

Sully didn't give me an opportunity to avoid thinking about my potential spelling boo-boo since his face and raised arms kept filling the screen as he scored goal after goal. It wasn't long before the ice was littered with a plethora of the new hats after three goals scored him another hat trick. Was his desire to be a hockey star so strong that he'd incriminate a witch to hide his angel status?

When the familiar thumping dance song erupted through the speakers during the break, I rolled my eyes. Despite being a newbie here, I recognized the song Donny, the beer vendor, considered his song. According to Grace, he used it as his ticket to fame and to coerce a few extra tips.

I folded my arms and looked at the corner of television screen that displayed Donny. He'd already set down his basket of beer in preparation for his dance moves. He stood waiting until the cameraman found him. He winked and then raised his arms, nodding his head as if people were clamoring to see his *manopausal* dance moves. He dropped his arms and then lifted and lowered one foot, and then the other.

I raised a brow. He looked like he was trying to make it to the restroom without an accident. After planting his feet, he put his hands on his waist and started gyrating in slow circles, gaining speed until I feared he might throw out a hip.

Instead of a hip, he reached up and pulled off his cap embellished with the number 69—my ever-present reminder of Sully's hat trick status. He swung it around as if riding a bucking bronco while standing close to the railing in case he lost his balance. His performance ended with him tossing his hat so the overhead lights reflected off his gleaming bald head. He caught the hat as it fell, and then gave an elaborate bow and final wink to the camera.

I'd seen his performance twice now, and already had it memorized, and was sure he waxed his skull to get it to shine brighter than a vamps' pearly whites.

I could easily take Donny on.

One benefit of being a cocktail waitress was having ample time to practice my dance moves. I claimed it was to keep my figure, but anyone who knew a lick about witches knew our metabolism rivaled a were's, so extra dancing wasn't necessary. I danced because I loved it.

Donny was a friendly enough guy, but the extra tips he made from his mediocre performance had me wishing I could show him how it was done. I could probably make more tips in that one minute than I would all night behind a bar.

10

I wiped the bar counter and glanced at the clock again with a sigh. Not much longer. I'd hoped to have figured out a plan to spring Grace by now. Then, she was so going to kill me. I hadn't been able to gauge exactly how furious she was in the short time I saw her, but I was sure there was going to be fury. She might even risk gaining a couple dark streaks in her pristine hair.

I dropped my bar rag to turn toward what I thought was a new customer.

Nope. Just Donny.

The beer vendor waddled the rest of the way up the stairs. When he caught my gaze, he put a little swagger in his step and jutted out his round belly as if it were a chiseled chest. I rolled my eyes. He acted as if he was the goddess's gift to females.

The man had to have a huge amount of self-confidence to feel so sure of himself while surrounded by beefy hockey players. No way could he come close to holding a candle. The thought of beefcake hockey players stirred the memory of Sully in the shower room. His image swam into my conscious.

Donny must've thought my dreamy look was directed at him. He arrived at the counter, leaned on it with one elbow, and then inched close enough to give me a wink and a whiff of stale perspiration. His perfect smile and full set of choppers might be the only asset he had over the players. Many were missing at least one tooth and I'd bet my best cauldron most had magical dental repair done.

"You like the show?" Donny winked.

I scowled when the pungent scent of garlic filled my nostrils.

Donny smiled as I waved my hand through the air to disperse the odor. I swore he gobbled garlic on purpose because he knew the vamps hated it and that the witches' overactive olfactory glands would be overwhelmed with the smell. "You call that dancing?"

I regretted the words as soon as I said them. Even though I hadn't been here long and didn't know half of the rules outlined in that ginormous book, I knew one thing. No one challenged Donny's dancing.

His brows pulled down and then rose. He folded

his arms to rest on the table his belly created. "Why, do you think you could do better?"

His smug expression told me he didn't think I could, and that he was amused by the thought. When I'd first met him, he'd boasted that his dance routine was a tradition. It was more like a bad habit the season ticket holders had to endure. The first time they might think Donny's dance was cute—a novelty. After that, it became a challenge to locate him in the arena when his tune began. Almost like a *where's Donny* game. Then it just offered a chance to sprint for the restroom before the game resumed.

I might be crappy at hair care spells and stink at skating, but by the goddess I could dance—and better than most.

"Pfft, of course I do." I hadn't meant to lace my comment with enough arrogance to turn Donny's bald head to the color of a ripe tomato, but there it was.

"You're on, *witch*." He turned and stalked away.

The way he said *witch* confirmed I'd created enemy number bazillion until infinity and then some. I shouldn't have challenged him, but I needed a diversion after all this stress. I'd failed at so many things lately that I needed a win.

Dancing? I could win this.

My current coworker, a thin vamp, raised her even

thinner brows until they disappeared underneath her purple bangs. Vamps weren't judged by the colors of their hair like a witch. Her purple weave was perfectly acceptable—except when I caught her washing it in the sink after accidentally dipping the ends in nacho cheese. That was not acceptable, and so not cool. "Challenging Donny was stupid," she said.

I'd done a lot of stupid things in my life, but I doubted challenging Donny to a dance-off was the stupidest. I'd just wanted to take his ego down a few pegs. Maybe he'd be inspired to add a few new moves into his routine to spare the season ticket holders the endless repetition.

My head snapped up when the familiar beat of one of my favorite tunes blared from the speakers. They were playing my jam. "It's on." I turned with a huge grin to the purple-haired vamp whose name I couldn't remember and asked, "Can you cover for me?"

"Don't tell me you're going to go through with this?" She shook her head, and her purple locks barely moved.

I nodded. Donny wouldn't be able to resist putting on his little show with this song.

"Sure. Go ahead. You better hope Lee doesn't catch you wasting more time," she said, in what sounded like a threat.

I took Burton having my back for granted. Here it seemed like everyone wanted to take a stab at it. This irritation fueled my fire to rip up the dance floor and mop it with Donny's shiny noggin.

Energized by the song, I vaulted over the bar, earning a startled glance from the name-I-couldn't-remember-bartender and a roll of her eyes. My sensible shoes let me emerge through the curtained area with enough speed to challenge a vamp. The jumbotron had Donny plastered on the screen as he started his signature dance moves.

I jogged down the steps until I was one aisle over from Donny and raised my hands to let the music fill me. My eyes dropped closed and I wiggled my fingers in the air, bracing my feet on the step. Falling and breaking a bone or two wouldn't be the best way to start off the dance challenge and was probably a bad idea all together.

The volume of the crowd increased. Either Donny had finally added some flourish to his routine, or more likely, the camera had spotted me. The announcer confirmed my suspicions. "It looks like Donny has a challenger!"

The corner of my lip quivered as I resisted the urge to smile. Instead, I cracked an eye. My image was magnified on the jumbotron. The camera flashed back to a very irritated looking Donny. He must not have thought I would take him up on the challenge. No time to dwell on Mr. Cranky Khakis; it was time to cut the rug—or crack the concrete if I couldn't maintain my perch on the step as I busted a move.

The volume of the music increased until the sound became almost deafening. I slowly moved my hips to the beat, closing my eyes, inhaling as if I could consume the musical chords until my skin vibrated to release the sound.

Music wasn't magic, but it felt like it to me.

The crowd clapped along to the beat. A quick glimpse displayed the screen volleying from Donny to me, splitting the image displayed between us.

I started to dance. Slowly at first, as the music filled me. In my mind I was no longer in the arena. My worries about clearing Grace's name, figuring out if Sully was friend or foe, and determining who was responsible for the blatant witch persecution—all of it faded. The roar of the crowd blended with the beat of the drums. My body felt fluid and one with the tune. My heart quickened with the pulse of the song. I smiled when people began to chant, "Go girl, go girl!" confirming I was securing my win.

A gasp emitted through the crowd and then silence fell.

They must be amazed by my stellar moves! I smiled

and increased the speed of my hips and shimmied my shoulders. I peeked at the jumbotron as the song reached its crescendo.

Mother of malt balls I was on fire! I mean literally. This wasn't good. Sparks of magic flew from my hips with each shake of my money maker in a freakish firework display. Why couldn't this happen at the club, where I could've secured my spot as dancing queen for the next decade? Even Donny had stopped to stare at me with revulsion.

The song stopped. A few lingering pops of magic fluttered from my hips to fizzle out on the ground along with my job—and any possibility of avoiding Ava's wrath. I'd publicly performed magic within the arena ... on video. This would certainly decrease my ability to offer much of a defense in what would appear as a blatant act of magical defiance.

Even though no winner was claimed, Donny clasped his hands together above his head and shook them in triumph. The silence of the room, and my stellar hearing, let me overhear some of his victory speech. "I don't need magic to make you spellbound with my dancing."

As security descended the steps toward me, the announcer sputtered about a popcorn sale and declared Rockin' Don as the winner in an attempt to distract the crowd from watching my arrest. I was smart enough not to resist on video and marched toward the waiting security guards while clinging to my remaining shreds of dignity.

I turned with my head held high. No real harm had been done. Besides, they had to admit my moves had been superior even before the unintentional magic display.

I scanned the crowd when I reached the top step, and the security guard took my elbow. My attention strayed to the ice. Sully had removed his helmet and stood with it tucked under his arm. He left the line of players and skated across the ice. The camera followed his progress, displaying a narrowing of his brows.

He looked up and our gazes locked. I shook my head, fearing he might be tempted to intervene. I didn't want him risking his career over my stupidity.

"Well, that didn't take long." Grace slumped on the couch as I joined her in the makeshift prison.

I winced at her lack of faith in my promise to get her released, even though she was right. "I, umm—"

Grace held up her hand. "Save it. I saw the whole thing." She pointed at the large screen projected against the glass enclosure. "You were entertaining."

"I'm sorry." I was supposed to save her. To rectify the situation I'd created. I'd only made a bad situation worse. I pushed my hands farther into my cotton pockets. The forgiving fabric must be to accommodate the arena food.

I turned to stare at the screen while struggling to come up with a better apology.

Grace followed my gaze to the television and shrugged. "It's hockey all the time." Her usual jubilant manner had departed, leaving her looking tired and defeated. "After being force fed a visual diet of hockey 24/7, even I'm getting sick of it." She inclined her head toward a video camera mounted in the corner of the room.

Everything we said and did was being observed. Grace was warning me that I'd better watch what I said before I made things worse—if that was possible.

I struggled to think of something to say, but most were things I didn't want recorded. Such as who was behind this? Why were they holding her at the arena? If they had any valid charges, they should have charged her and released her until sentencing. But these were stupid rules of the arena, not law. They had no right.

I held this inside as the tension in the room became suffocating. "So how was I?" I shimmied my hips. No worries about any magic sparks in here, with the anti-magic enforcements.

She smiled weakly. "Rockin' Don didn't stand a chance. He didn't know who he was up against."

I plopped on the couch beside her and enveloped her in a hug before she could protest. I whispered in her ear. "I'm so sorry. This is all my fault."

Grace pulled away and nodded. "You're darn right it is. You should've known better than to pick your favorite song to show off your dance moves. I heard every beat." She tapped her ear. "You know how *witches* have stellar hearing." She stared at me. "But there was no chance as a *witch* that you could contain accidentally letting off a spark or two with that dance. Right, *witch*?" She looked to the camera again.

I opened my mouth to protest about her repeatedly referring to me as a witch like it was a bad thing and then followed her gaze instead. Either she'd become a bit feeble minded while sitting in this cell or more likely, she was trying to tell me something. I raised my brows. Had she just confirmed my suspicions about the barrier? Was a witch responsible? It would be disappointing to confirm that one of our own kind would do so much to harm the reputation of witches.

I glanced at the screen and then sighed. They repeatedly showed my image shooting up the arena with magical sparks. "I did rock some awesome dance moves. Those magic sparks would've been fabulous at the club. Just my luck the first time I get a dance ramped up to that level I'm at an anti-magic facility."

Grace shook her head with a slight smile.

Without the music playing in the background, the small frame in the upper right corner of the newsfeed featuring me that was shrunk by the newscaster's head made it look as if I was attacking the audience with my hexed hips. It made the situation seem more sinister than a simple dance off.

I winced.

That was exactly what Ava would see on the news. "Ava is going to be so ticked off."

"No doubt." Grace nodded, doing nothing to alleviate my concern.

I looked around the room that was a voyeur's dream. The open floor plan and glass enclosure was discomforting. I couldn't imagine how Grace felt. "Is there no privacy in here?"

"Not much. I can request the privacy screen, and it's always conjured for dressing, toileting and bathing, but that's about it. They want to make sure I'm not doing magic when they're not looking, or when I'm supposed to be sleeping. I don't know why they worry; there's a magic guard enacted around the whole place anyway. I couldn't so much as fix my hair.

Believe me, I tried." She pointed to her chestnut hair that now had a layer of frizz I'd never seen on her normally lustrous locks. The disarray confirmed she'd tried to escape with a spell.

"This is more than a little overreacting; it's barbaric. It's just a hockey game." I frowned and bit back my retort at Grace's sharp look. *Privacy screen? Magic guard?* There had to be a witch involved. No other species could produce that, plus Grace was being punished ridiculously for a minor spell. This had to be someone with a grudge. But who would have a grudge with Grace?

I knew the answer to that—*no one.*

But if I thought of myself, that list might be a little harder to narrow down. If Grace couldn't spell her way out of here, there was no way I could do anything to help. "I'm sure you're wishing you got stuck with Ava instead of me."

"Like that would ever happen." She silenced at my raised brow and then shrugged. "Nothing we can do now but wait for her."

🌸 11 🌸

I looked around the small room. I could only hope Jasper was okay. He could take care of himself, but with no witches working in the arena, it made me worry. The paranormals here didn't share any love for witches, so they surely wouldn't feel much for a witch's cat. Even if Jasper wasn't officially my familiar yet, they'd think he was. Thank the goddess Gran wasn't here to see this. "How will Ava know where to find you? Umm ... us?"

"She's resourceful." Grace looked at me meaningfully and enunciated each word. "We've been keeping in touch."

I frowned at the odd change in her behavior. Perhaps being caged in for this long was wreaking havoc with her mentally, or they'd done something to her. I scanned Grace from head to toe and detected nothing amiss. Although her baggy clothes could conceal all kinds of stuff. "Where's your jersey?"

"They took it. Said it was evidence," she said and cast her eyes down.

Guilt tightened its grip on me; causing Grace to lose her beloved jersey was yet another way I'd wronged her. I lowered my voice to a whisper. "How are you keeping in touch with Ava?" She was in an inescapable room, and unless she'd figured out some kind of mental telepathy—I'd heard about a spell for that—she might be getting a bit mental.

Grace tilted her head ever so slightly toward the edge of the closet cabinet in one of the far corners of the enclosure.

Okay, it was the mental part.

Was she implying she'd stashed my sister in the closet?

I shrugged.

Anything was possible in this upside-down situation. Although I had my doubts about the closet. Ava was claustrophobic. I'd have heard her screaming from the arena.

But Grace kept nodding in that direction and seemed to want me to check it out.

To humor her, I stood and started toward the closet. She grabbed my shoulder, halting me. "Go slow." She hugged me as she leaned close to my ear to whisper, "Don't worry. He's friendly."

She pulled away and then nodded again, as if convincing herself of the answer. That, or she'd lost the ability to halt her bobbing head.

"Okay." I looked at the closet again. Friendly? What was that supposed to mean? The oak cabinet didn't look threatening. It looked like a closet. The stained wood was ordinary looking, with an elaborate molding on the corners. I drew my brows down. One of the edges looked darker than the other, almost black—and lumpy. They must've had a crappy carpenter finish the job, or a magical accident could have burnt it.

I approached the closet and caught movement out of the corner of my eye. I halted and tensed. "What in a *jack-o-lantern's smile* is that?"

"Shh, keep your voice down. You'll scare him." Grace spoke through gritted teeth as she glanced toward the camera. A career as a ventriloquist clearly wasn't in her future.

"Him? What about me? I didn't think those things existed anymore." The gargoyle shifted so I could see his face as he stretched and spread his wings before folding them underneath again. He looked somewhat like a big bat petrified into stone.

Grace stepped closer, and we both stared at the

closet if indecisive regarding what to wear. "I think he was hers. You know, the one in charge."

"So why is he talking, or whatever he's doing with my sister, and how is he doing it?" My whisper was harsh, and I hoped it wouldn't be overheard on whatever kind of monitoring devices they were using. Why wasn't Grace worrying about them hearing? "Should we be talking about this here?"

"It's okay, we're close enough. Freddie can shield our conversation from prying ears. Right, Freddie?" She smiled up at her lumpy companion.

"Freddie?" The name kind of suited the hideous stonelike creature only a mother could love, or a witch trapped in solitary for too long. Or Grace. She loved every animal. I did too, but a gargoyle?

"It's short for EggFreddie. He prefers Freddie." She squeezed my shoulder.

The gargoyle nodded and flashed what might have been a grin except the pointed teeth looked a bit more terrifying than friendly.

"How did he get in here, or out?"

"Through the skylight. Much of the stuff in this area operates on solar power rather than being connected with the rest of the arena. I assume they didn't want it to be easy to locate," Grace replied.

I glanced up, for the first time realizing there was a skylight far above us that provided most of the lighting. Not easy to locate was right. All that time it took me to find the room and then I stumbled upon it by accident.

My attention returned to the corner of the closet, and I found it matching the other side—no stone-shaped jack-o-lantern-faced critter resided there.

"Where did he go?" I pulled my limbs closer, as if he might decide to perch on my shoulder for an eerie introduction.

"He'll only let you see him when he wants to," she said.

"Great. An invisible creepy critter."

Grace poked my shoulder. "Hey. He's my friend and he's sensitive. He wasn't treated very nicely for the last couple hundred years, and it takes a while to earn his trust."

"Couple hundred years? How long do those things live for?"

"Those *things* were probably around long before us and don't like to be insulted. Quit calling him a thing. Apologize to Freddie," she said.

I rolled my eyes. We were trapped in a solitary cell and Grace was worried about me minding my manners with a reptilian creature. "Why? He's not here to hear my apology."

"Yes, he is. In fact, he's waiting for you to apologize." She nudged me and pointed toward the floor.

I jumped and swallowed the reflexive scream rising in my throat when I discovered the little stone oddity wrapped around my leg, clinging to my calf like a lone boot. He stared up at me with huge, voluminous eyes. I had to admit, he did look as if I'd hurt his feelings. Who knew a stone had feelings?

"Umm ... Freddie. I'm sorry. I didn't mean to insult you." I glanced to Grace, and she gestured for me to continue, even though I felt ridiculous. "It's just that I've never met a gargoyle before, and you startled me." I didn't add that he was freaking me out at that moment by acting as if he'd morphed into part of my attire.

Grace bent to pat his head and he closed his eyes in satisfaction. "He's desperate for attention."

"How do you know?"

She let out a slow sigh. "Well, besides his expression of rapture that makes it obvious, he told me."

"He talks?" I stared down at him, hoping he found me more friend than foe and didn't decide to take a taste of my thigh.

Grace shrugged. "When he wants to. I don't think the other witch permitted him to. She didn't like being shown up by something older and wiser that was only a fraction of her size. At least that's how Freddie sees it."

Freddie nodded and climbed a few inches higher

on my leg. I resisted the impulse to shake him off. "Does he have to cling to my leg like that?"

"It's part of how he camouflages himself against the camera. They only see our clothing, or the object he's attached to. If he's on the floor, or somewhere else by himself, then he's more obvious as a slight discrepancy on the camera."

We both raised our attention to the little camera in the corner. Neither of us had committed more of a crime than being a witch. Magic was part of our nature. This situation stunk of someone's personal agenda. Was there a witch that one of us had wronged, and was now seeking revenge? Or was this an elaborate cover-up to distract from the fact that there was an angel on the team?

There had to be something more that I could do than wait for Ava to rescue us.

"This is how you're communicating with Ava? Through a gargoyle?" I couldn't conceal my surprise, nor my humor at the thought of my sister working with a gargoyle. She had enough trouble accepting my dog, then when I adopted Jasper and explained how we communicated, I think she gave up any remaining hope that I'd ever fit into her definition of normal.

The thought of having a mini spy was an alluring one. Although I didn't think this was the true purpose of a gargoyle. It was what Freddie had been reduced to. Perhaps there were more gargoyles around and I hadn't noticed them. Freddie sure was easy to miss if you didn't know what you were looking for.

I joined Grace in the weird ventriloquist manner of conversing and leaned closer to her. "Who is the head witch here; did Freddie tell you?"

Grace shook her head. "He can't."

"Why not? It seems like she doesn't treat him well. You think he'd be flapping his gums to get rid of her." I looked down. Freddie was gone from my leg. A quick scan located him back on the corner of the cabinet as if he'd never left.

"No, I mean he can't. He's under a spell that prohibits him from speaking her name. He's tried, believe me." Grace lowered to the couch, and I sat beside her.

That would be convenient, especially if my memory served right; gargoyles were associated more with demons than other paranormal. Surely this stony critter wasn't covering up for a demon?

The exterior door opened with a loud creak, and we both jumped to our feet. I squinted but couldn't discern anything or anyone out of the darkness surrounding our brightly lit room.

The fall of multiple footsteps echoed.

Several sounded like heavy boots, and one a light padding. "Of course, Lee would be involved."

Grace looked to me, but I didn't have time to explain about my new—and most likely former—supervisor.

Lee hurried his narrow behind to the forefront of the group. He was beaming from ear to ear. His fangs cut into his lower lip in his excitement. I didn't think anything could've made him happier than seeing me behind magic-barring glass. I'm not sure that I ever made an enemy faster without knowing what set off his stink meter.

Grace leaned to my ear. "I think that's her right-hand man."

"Figures." I snorted. "Although calling him a man is a bit generous."

The outer door opened and cast a panel of light across the floor. The tall, cloaked figure made her way across the floor toward the enclosure. The build and sway to the walk implied it was probably a woman. I nudged Grace, as if she wasn't staring at the approaching figure as well. "This must be her."

I wasn't sure why I felt the need to inform Grace of what was apparent. I tensed and found myself face to face with a witch. A very cantankerous one at that.

"Well, well, well. What do we have here? Two

little peas in a pod." Gin-and-juice Gloria leaned close to the glass and stared in as if we were in a petri dish. In a way, we were. She wrinkled her nose in disgust.

"But you're a witch," I blurted. To confirm that one of our own was behind all the rules about magic in the arena was infuriating. Although I hated to put myself, or any of the witches I cared for, into the same category as Gloria. She gave all witches a bad name.

Grace's vehement anger distracted me from my surprise. "You couldn't spin a spell to save your life. That's why you hide behind layers of magic binding and rules. Because you know the rest of us can show you up."

I drew my gaze from Gloria to gape at mild-mannered Grace. "What? How?" I was still flummoxed that Gloria had waltzed in, and Grace seemed to have figured out much more about her motive in a short time.

Grace poked me in the arm to stir me from my stupor. "Despite her appearance of looking destitute most of the time, Gloria has big bucks. Not that you'd know from the paltry tips she leaves at the club, but I'd heard a witch owned part of the arena. It makes sense now. She's privy to all the areas in the arena and the players. The no-magic rule was made and enforced by her since she didn't want any competition. She was a silent partner—until now."

I gaped at Grace, and she shrugged and said, "I just put it together. We had all the pieces of the puzzle but didn't know how, or who, they fit."

It still didn't make sense to me. How could Gloria have known I'd go to the game, let alone cast a spell over nacho cheese? Wasn't I the one who'd set this in motion?

Gloria rolled her good eye while the other one remained locked in place, staring at us. "I'm not one of you. I may have spelling in my blood and be born a witch, but I can assure you I do not consider myself to be anything like you heathens."

She strutted in front of the glass enclosure in a long black gown that hung off her skeletal frame as if she were a clothes hanger in the store. Her collarbones pressed against her skin, longing to break free from their confinement. The long sleeves of the gown belled at the ends and pooled at her elbow when she raised her hand to gesture. "What's one, or two, less witches for this world? I'm working on my own coven of pureblood witches that follows righteous beliefs. Beliefs that maintain the reputation we've been trying to shed for ages. Witches should be feared."

I was still mentally catching up. Gloria's ego might've kept her alive for years, but her anger kept her motivated. That and layers upon layers of hair-spray and gin.

"You see, this is how it's going to work. Your hockey hero is going to have to come to your rescue. He gets to save two witches for the price of one. Surely that will mend his broken conscious, huh? Well, that's not going to happen. His fame places blame on a witch for illegally performing magic. He's irked the witches and the supernatural community and struck fear into the hearts of mortals. People like rules. They don't feel safe when they're broken. Sully will be responsible for ruining two innocent lives. I doubt that will bode well for earning back those wings." She tiled her head to the side and made a pouty face. "Too bad he won't find out his role in your fate until it's too late."

Grace's hand clap broke through the silence "Wouldn't that be convenient? Getting rid of a few more witches to help you rise above? You won't get away with it."

Gloria didn't turn toward Grace, but instead she focused on me. Her smile was slow and predatory. "This is working out exactly as I planned. I'm sure your sweet-as-saccharin twin won't be able to resist getting you out of this mess, will she? I get sick of hearing your whining about the crap in your life, how you're responsible, but Ava has to fix all your magical messes. You won't be a huge loss to the magic community. They know you're a bumbling amateur who should have no right to a broomstick, but they'll mourn Ava the super witch. She's done nothing but try to raise up the magic community and you'll be responsible for her downfall."

My eyes widened as comprehension dawned.

It wasn't me she wanted. It never was.

It was Ava, and worse, Sully.

Silence loomed heavy after the group left the room until Freddie revealed himself to us. Grace stared at him intently.

"Is he saying something?"

Grace knelt and placed her hand on Freddie's head. "He said he'll go warn Sully."

"How's he going to do that? Sully won't pay attention to him." I wouldn't have seen the gargoyle myself if Grace hadn't pointed him out.

Grace met my gaze. "You have to want to see Freddie. You have to have believe in magic."

I looked through the glass to the dark dismal room. "No wonder no one noticed him in this place."

We'd barely settled back on the couch after Gloria departed when the exterior door creaked open again.

"Now what?" I asked.

Two large weres preceded the woman cast in shadows behind their bulk and blocked my initial ability to determine who it might be.

Deep down, I knew who it was.

It wasn't Gloria, the witch in charge of this charade, but a guest. I would've preferred Gloria again; despite how I'd waited for this, and wanted this, it felt worse.

When one were broke from their little pack to stop at the talk box and press a few buttons to enable sound through the room, I got my first glimpse at her. It confirmed my suspicions.

I knew I should have been relieved, but I dreaded the moment her eyes locked with mine almost more than seeing Lee here. Ava.

I was so dead.

Not dead in the *never living again* way, or even the *vamp way of living the undead life*. More like suffering endless agony from being thrust into purgatory to continuously repent for my sins—and this sin was one I'd be repenting for a long time, no matter what the outcome.

I braced myself for my fate and looked into the eyes shaped exactly like mine. "Hello, Ava."

"Hello, Sis." Ava smiled, but I saw the steel behind her gaze. Obviously, she was saving the lecture for later when there weren't so many prying ears and eyes surrounding her. It was sure to be a doozy.

"*Sister?*" Lee's initial excitement faded as he glanced between the two of us.

There was some resemblance, but you had to look for it, and Ava's polished suit and professional demeanor didn't align with any of my personality. I didn't know what Ava had told him to gain entrance to the fortress of solitude, but clearly, she had bent the truth a little along the way.

Too bad she hadn't figured that out *before* I'd joined Grace.

The whiny vamp turned to Ava. "I thought you were here to grill her?"

The way he said it implied that he'd already envisioned me on a spit roasting above the flames. It seemed he was getting way too much satisfaction from the disturbing image, too.

"I am, but not like you're thinking, and not with all of you hulking hordes of testosterone hovering around me." She turned ever so slightly to face them. Her words were laced with a sugary sweetness that only Grace and I could discern for what it really was. Ava was pissed, and thank the goddess it wasn't only directed at me.

I detected just when the tipping point of control shifted.

It wasn't magic; it was just who she was, so there was no way to resist. Believe me, I'd faced down Ava's withering stare more times than I could count, and I never won the battle.

Luckily, these dudes realized their fate pretty quick.

Later they would probably claim it had been magic and that they couldn't resist or retaliate. It was the only way many a male saved their fragile ego when this tiny wisp of a woman cowed them with a glance.

The weres paled, and Lee stumbled back a step,

making it appear as if Ava had cast a spell—but she hadn't needed to. Her ability to gain the upper hand in almost any conversation with barely saying a word was what made any subject in the areas of justice and law a natural fit for her.

You couldn't pinpoint what convinced you she was right—*always* right—but you couldn't find the words to argue, either. Suddenly, all protests sounded feeble and lame when she impaled you with a look.

"Go ahead and let Grace out. That's all for now." Ava let her gaze linger for a few seconds on each man until they backed away.

Lee sputtered a few times in protest as his gaze darted between Ava and me, probably uncertain how the situation had gone sideways. He was going to be in a vat of trouble with his boss, Gloria, although he appeared prepared to face that rather than Ava's silent, unspoken threat.

He rushed forward and unlocked the cell door, muttering his displeasure the entire time but unwilling to challenge Ava.

"Sorry, Sis. I'm still working on your release. It was easy to prove Grace had nothing to do with the spell. Now we have to prove that the spell was unintentional and not meant to impact the hockey game."

I grimaced.

There had been intention behind the spell, but it was only to get rid of the nacho cheese.

Ava gave me one final glance. "Don't worry, Marissa. This is bogus. I'm getting the facts to find out who is behind this charade. I have an inside source, and James Stone as a consultant, and someone will pay the price."

James Stone? I was surprised the pale P.I. was assisting. After being cursed to resemble a ghost I wouldn't think helping a witch would rank high on his agenda.

As Grace exited the cell, she gave me a pat on the arm. "Don't worry. I'm sure Ava will take care of it. It can't be long."

I nodded. "Please find Jasper before you go. Make sure he's okay," I said. I deserved this time alone to think about how my blunder had caused this mess.

Once they left, three guards came to stand inside the doors. A flicker of red across their eyes had me suspecting they were demons. Gloria must have had all kinds on her payroll. As if they were even necessary.

"Hey guys, don't you think you're overdoing it? It was a nacho cheese spell. Not a nuclear bomb."

One of the guards had the nerve to make my life more miserable by insisting that he had to bind me to the chair.

"Listen, big guy. It's not like I have any hope of escaping."

He ignored my protests and continued with the ties. Either they had more faith in my magical abilities than my sister, or they were expecting another visitor.

I didn't turn when Gloria approached. The scent of dark magic gave her away. "Back so soon?"

Her smug expression and the way she looked down her long pointy nose at me said more than any words she could have spoken. She thought she was better than me—undeserving of her time.

But it wasn't me I was concerned with as much as what she'd put Grace through.

Gloria touched my hair, twirling the black strands through her fingers. "You fret so much about what other people think instead of embracing all you can be. Why do people care so much about what someone thinks? We're all dark on the inside. Most try to hide their true nature."

I pulled away, prompting her to drop my hair, but not without giving me a tug on my scalp first.

Gloria reclined in the chair and crossed one long, gangly leg over the other, studying her nails. "Do you have any idea of how many weak witches I've dealt with in my long lifetime?"

She acted as if she was pondering the question,

her expression thoughtful as she ticked off her fingers one by one. Then, she shook her head. "Too many to count."

She stood and glided across the room with the long train of her black dress trailing behind her, swishing against the floor. "Anybody can be born a witch. It's those who rise and embrace their heritage that stand above the rest. Coming into one's own usually requires a little bloodshed along the way, and most people are squeamish about that. The whole wanting to fit in with the rest of the paranormal and mortals is pathetic. *Fit in?* They should all be bowing down to us."

I sighed. "Despite forcing me to be your captive audience, I'm not in the mood for a lecture." I'd always disliked Gloria, but this was taking it to the next level. Anger built within me for how she'd wronged Grace, whatever she was doing to Sully, and how she had threatened Ava. "You have no right to hold me here."

She shot across the room to stop inches from my face.

I felt immobilized without the use of a spell.

What kept me frozen was my own fury. The tremors running through my body were almost painful to contain. The fear that if I released any of

my anger, I'd come undone. That I might spontaneously combust in a shower of magic.

Maybe that was her goal.

She wanted to bring out the worst in me, so I
would be more like her.

I couldn't let her.

Her smile was predatory. The low lighting cast
shadows over her face, highlighting all the sharp,
angry angles. "Let it out. Be the witch you were born
to be."

"No." I wouldn't give her the satisfaction of arguing
with her, of feeding her need to fuel my rage. "You're just
an evil witch filled with hate." I winced at my inability to
put my anger into words stronger than those of a child.

Gloria laughed and touched my cheek. I jerked
away.

She continued with her unsolicited lecture. "The
demons are as bad as the rest of them. They won't let
a witch in amongst them, even when we prove we can
do their job better than they can. They're intimidated
—*afraid*. As they should be. You think that glorified
doorman to the damned is your friend?" She shook
her head. "Don't humor yourself. He's doing his job.
Personally, my thought is that you entertain him. I
love seeing you slipping further away from being a
do-gooder witch. You might not see it happening, but

I do. Just compare yourself to your sister. Not even close, am I right?"

I looked away, fearing she'd read my thoughts of inferiority when it came to my sister.

Gloria continued without waiting for my response. "The demons know how to do it. They don't care about anything. Get rid of the soul, and then you have your race of super witches. All I wanted was to find out how the demons managed to get rid of those pesky feelings that hold us back from having it all. No more worrying about others and feeling guilty or weighed down with indecision. But they wouldn't share an iota of their secrets with a witch."

I pulled at the bindings, but they held tight. Even if I could have freed myself, I wasn't sure what I would do, and then I'd have to deal with the demons outside the enclosure.

Gloria glanced at my pathetic struggles and rolled her eyes. "With each spell you cast, you go a little darker. You might think you can tell how evil someone is by the color of their hair. Well, I can tell you; there's a lot more that I see on their tarnished souls. I bet yours has seen better days." She held up a few locks of her hair and let them fall to join the rest. The color—a sleek black—was darker than the darkest night. "Why hide the truth? Stop fooling yourself and set yourself free."

She held out her arms. "Together, we can rule this town, this country, this *world* if we choose to. Join my army of witches as we take our rightful place as the superior supernatural race. No more rules binding us of our magic. No more angels and demons claiming they can do it better than us, or the rest of the mismatched mongrels making up this world."

I closed my eyes and took a deep, calming breath, thinking about all the people in my life.

Sure, there were times when they did me wrong, and times when I drove them crazy, but they still loved me even if they didn't always show it well, no matter what kind of bloodline their family tree drew from.

I thought about Gloria and saw the vast emptiness that surrounded her.

That she had built out of her anger and hate.

She'd put up those walls and refused to let anyone in.

That was no life.

My muscles relaxed, and my anger began to soothe—almost like a cool stream of water running over my body. I let the rage ride away with the current and dissipate, unclenching my fists and allowing my fingers to relax. "I'll never be like you."

"Sometimes, it's not the path we choose, but the choices we make that provide the end result." She turned to walk away. "Remember, those choices aren't always for us, but about what we're willing to sacrifice."

Gloria exited and shut the enclosure, stopping in front of the glass to say, "Think about my offer."

The sound of the outer door opening had me dropping my head back and closing my eyes. "Not again," I said with a groan.

I couldn't even get any peace and quiet while in this so-called seclusion. Surely, Gloria had better things to do than flap her gums at me, like report back to whoever was in charge. I refused to believe that wacky witch had enough influence to cow the SHL.

"Stop the presses, hold your horses, or whatever corny expression serves you to leave this wily, and a bit whiney, witch alone," Joe said to the guards as he sashayed into the room.

He had one hand on his hip and the other raised like he was giving a parade wave to his adoring fans. His skintight black leather outfit, complete with stiletto heeled boots and a clingy fuchsia sweater, announced his arrival better than any bullhorn.

Joe marched right by the stunned guards, opened the enclosure without any effort, and came in to stand beside me. He placed a hand on my shoulder and gave it a squeeze. I looked up into his heavily lined, retro-blue shadowed eyes.

Every girl wanted a knight in shining armor to come riding to their rescue, but I hadn't expected a peculiar hairdresser in black leather.

"Joe?"

Even though I'd come to expect the unexpected from Joe and appreciated the magic and finesse he had with my hair, I didn't think his talents extended to jail-breaks. Just when I'd resigned myself to sitting in solitude to dwell on all my wrongdoings and keep myself out of everyone else's harm's way, Joe came to the rescue.

He patted my head and pulled a coil of my curls to examine with a grimace. "Girl, if you don't get your hiney out of the clinker soon and let me reduce the damage to this hairdo, it's gonna be a hopeless case."

"You're here to save my hair?" The thought was ridiculous and hilarious, even though his comment about the imminent hopelessness of my hair sent a shiver up my spine and a tightening around my heart.

"Well, that's one thing. Besides telling these fire-

and-brimstone bludgeoning jerks that there's no way you've cast any kind of nasty spell, or I'd know it from the looks of your hair. It might look like crap on a cracker—"

"Hey!" I'd had a rough enough day without having to endure insults.

He shrugged. "Well, it does. But it's looked like that, complete with your big, black stripe of shame, for some time now. There's no way they can try to blame you for something that would've easily shown up, and I would've known about it."

He shook his head and clucked his tongue as he ran his fingers through my mane like a monkey searching for fleas. There was a yearning in his gaze that displayed his longing to get his hands on my tresses. "I've been battling the beast that is your hair for more time than I care to admit. A hairstylist is only as good as his work, you know."

The biggest dude took a step toward the cell, blocking the exit. "It doesn't matter what you have to say about her hair or whether there's evidence of spelling. If the boss wants her to stay, then here she stays." A red light flickered across his eyes and faded out.

I leaned toward Joe, whispering even though nothing was secret with the supernatural hearing of most in the room. "Joe. These aren't your ordinary bullies."

Joe had a reputation as a tough guy in the salon. Perhaps his brash nature had gone to his head. He was going to end up getting us both killed. Or maimed enough that it would take serious spelling by a better witch than me—so we could show our faces in public.

"I know. They're a bunch of jerks." Joe raised his voice on the last word and did a little swirly circle with his head to make his point. Just like him to make a tenuous situation go from bad to absolutely horrible with a head shake.

"No, Joe. I mean they're not what you think," I said. I wasn't sure if I was supposed to know these guys were demons, but I'd seen the signs before; for goodness sake, I was around one every day. The difference was that, believe it or not, Burton had more manners than these hooligans.

Joe rolled his eyes and gave a flutter of the long lashes I was sure had to be magically enhanced despite his adamant denial. "You mean they're not demons?"

He pulled me up out of my chair as if the binds weren't even there.

With a glance, I noticed that they weren't, but I

had no idea what happened to them. "What? Where?"

I stumbled alongside Joe like a resistant child as I pondered what had become of the bindings. Joe's casual comment settled in my brain. "You knew? What do you know about dealing with demons?"

Joe sighed. "Can't you ever just trust me and go with the flow? So many questions. I swear you have the curiosity of a two-year-old. I know more than you ever want to about demons."

The three thugs in question lined up in front of us like some kind of muscle curtain blocking our path. Huge biceps created more of a barrier than any fence or magical binding ever could. "I don't think they're going to let us through, Joe."

If Joe had broken the magic barriers surrounding the enclosure, I could've stirred a few potions; I loved the challenge of using hodgepodge ingredients and had been known to make a potion out of thin air, a paperclip, and a toenail clipping.

I could've cast a spell or two if I didn't mind adding more black streaks to my hideous hair, or if I had the gumption in me.

But I didn't.

I didn't even think of trying. I just didn't care.

The solitary confinement did briefly keep me out

of trouble and prevent me from meddling in anyone else's life for at least five minutes.

The men moved a step closer, standing tall in a threatening gesture as they towered over us. It worked, as I found it more than a little intimidating in my current state of desperation and despair with only a scrawny, well-versed-in-fashion, hairdresser to serve as my hero.

Two of the three men were bald, so it wasn't like Joe could promise them his magic fingers for their tresses unless he knew how to spell some new locks from scratch. That spell remained as elusive as one for folding and maintaining a neat, fitted sheet.

"Joe?"

"They'll move." Joe's smile was slow and sexy as he cocked his head to the side in challenge. "Wait till they get a load of me."

It wasn't as if he could whip out the can of hairspray that was ever-present on his hip like some kind of holster equipped with aerosol spray.

I frowned.

Well, perhaps he could spray their red flickering eyes once or twice to slow them down if he was so intent on escaping with me as his damsel in distress.

Something bumped me from behind, and I stumbled forward a bit before Joe tightened his grip to keep me from face planting on the floor. "Watch yourself, girl."

I turned to see what had assaulted me and dropped right on my behind when all the strength suddenly left my legs.

Two enormous black wings had sprouted from Joe's back and extended the length of the room, elevating his fashionable outfit to that of a celestial ready to kick butt.

"What the ..."

Joe waved me off. "I know, I know. Save your fawning for later. Not everyone can handle all of this." He gestured from his head, which was adorned with a wig coiffed about six inches tall, past his wings, and down to his pointy boots.

"Girl, you can stop staring at me like I just grew wings and a tail. Oh, wait a minute. I had the wings; you just didn't know about them."

"But you're ..." How could I say that I didn't imagine an angel would come equipped with enough sarcasm to sink a ship and more attitude than his tiny frame looked capable of maintaining?

Apparently, I didn't have to say it. "You sure are something," I said.

This helped explain more about Joe's heritage, but it still left me with plenty of questions.

"Time for some angel cake, boys," one of the demons said with a smirk.

The demons had retreated a few steps but seemed to have regained their confidence, and a look of eager anticipation filled their faces. "Like one little ol' angel is going to scare us off."

"What about two?"

When the door slammed shut, we all focused on the shirtless man whose glorious bare chest rivaled that of a god, in my book. Like a clown car packed with a seemingly impossible amount of people, Sully's wings grew and expanded until they reached his mid-thigh. Once they stopped growing, they pressed out to the side and lifted in a gorgeous display until they almost reached the walls.

They were massive.

Impressive.

And completely breathtaking.

He filled the room as his wings expanded, and the three demons were left caught in the middle of the angels.

Sully tucked his wings slightly so he could turn to face me and then allowed them to unfold to their full extent. He presented an intimidating figure. One that would make many confess to their wrongdoings and beg for forgiveness.

I couldn't pinpoint the rationale that would

prompt this action, but there was something about him standing still and letting the wings speak louder than any words.

"Sully?"

"Freddie told me," he said.

As if that explained everything.

I knew he was an angel, but what the heck? Was everyone in my life some kind of secret supernatural superhero?

"It would be helpful if someone would've filled me in on the celestial pool I've been soaking in, although obviously none of your goody-goodness has worn off on me. Next thing you're going to tell me is that Burton is an angel too," I said.

Joe and Sully exchanged a look, and all three demons stilled.

"What?" I barked out laugh and then sobered. "No way is Burton an angel."

"No, not exactly. Not now." Joe rolled his eyes so much I feared he could see out of the back of his head. "Here you go with the twenty questions thing again."

As the only female in this tight circle of men, I felt as if I might soon drown in testosterone as each tried to intimidate the other. My only potential competition for the estrogen was Joe, and I thought he might just borrow it from time to time.

As I stood back up, the bigger demon leaned toward me, causing both Joe and Sully to move closer. "You know Burton?"

I brushed myself off and stood in front of the beast of a man, tilting back to be able to gain eye contact. "Of course, I do. I work with him every day. I know him about as well as anyone can know my silent, but potentially deadly, *friend*."

The demons exchanged a look and mumbled amongst themselves when I emphasized the word "friend." I couldn't imagine that word came up too often in a sentence about Burton.

I caught the words, *boss, mouthy witch*, and *up the creek* before they turned and abruptly made their way to the door, as if they weren't about to begin a super-natural showdown between angels and demons. I was relieved since I was sure to be burnt in the crossfire of that battle.

"What happened? They changed their mind? I guess I'm free to go," I said with a shrug. It wasn't like Joe was giving me much of a choice, but the demons' hasty departure was odd. "I would've brought Burton up earlier if I'd have known his name had any pull. Guess I didn't need you boys after all. What is Burton, then?"

"A demon," Joe supplied with a roll of his eyes.

"I know, but he's not like those guys."

Joe glanced from Sully to me and then replied, "No. He's worse."

I didn't know what Joe meant, and I wasn't sure I wanted to explore it. "But he's such a nice, quiet guy."

When both angels looked at me, I realized I'd delivered the standard line after someone discovered that their neighbor wasn't the sweet dude that they thought, and instead had a vat in the basement he cooked up corpses in and wore their skin to the holiday party.

Sully ran his gaze over Joe.

Both men still stood in tense postures with their wings rising above them as if they were about to begin some weird rooster fight over disputed territory. As I studied their wings, they shimmered slightly, and appeared more shadow-like than real. Almost as if they were an illusion.

I extended my hand and noted the slight tremble in my arm. "May I?"

Sully nodded. "You'll have to do so before they complete their metamorphosis into shadows."

The white wings were rapidly fading to a black fog.

They felt soft under my fingers and then seemed to pass through them as they made themselves appropriate for the world's view. Their consistency flowed through my fingers with the smooth feel of a waterfall until his back looked as if they'd never been there at all. I might've thought I'd imagined the whole thing.

Since I was in between the men, I wasn't sure what my role was.

I stepped a few feet away from both as they continued with some silent standoff where they stared each other down, almost daring the other to blink.

My bets were on Sully in this round since he was the only one of the two not wearing some kind of super enhanced eyelashes that had to get irritating, or at least mess with your vision, after a while.

"Hey, Joe." Sully relaxed his wings, and Joe followed suit until both had tucked their wings completely out of sight.

I looked to Joe, and then to Sully. "Wait. Do you guys know each other? Someone better fill me in here on what the hell, or heaven, is going on."

"Not hell. But close," Joe said in his annoying way where he spoke in sarcastic riddles, assuming we had a clue as to what he was talking about. "It all depends on what Sully chooses, and if it's enough for a fallen angel to earn back his grace."

🎋 14 🎋

I closed my eyes with a sigh as Joe worked his magic on my hair after waiting a week until he could squeeze me in an appointment. Now that Grace and I were out of that ridiculous lockup, we'd yet to determine what Gloria's role was, and ensure she paid for her actions. Most likely, Ava, and James Stone, would take care of that while I dug into the situation with Sully.

And of course, there was still Joe's missing hat to contend with.

"So ... an angel?"

Joe paused from caring for my hair to cock a hip. "What did you think? That all angels were goody goodies? Angels are warriors, girl. Don't you read your history books?"

"No."

Like he had to ask that question. Joe knew me well enough by now to know that studying wasn't my strong point.

I bet Gran would've had the answers.

I hadn't realized how much I relied on her vat of knowledge until she took off for that cruise.

He waved me off. "Geez, Louise, what did you think I was?"

I thought Joe could have been a lot of things, but *angel* never crossed my mind. I avoided informing him that I'd speculated he could have been one of any number of underworld creatures staked out on earth as a svelte hairdresser, and instead tried to distract him with a compliment. "I guess that's why you have the magic touch with my hair."

"I don't need any magic." He rolled his eyes so far back he looked in danger of having a seizure and tossed a hand up, drawing the stink eye from several of the other witches in the salon who probably assumed he was mocking our heritage.

Perhaps he was.

It was hard to tell with Joe.

After pausing for dramatic flair, he resumed working on my hair to make it so glorious its unearthly glow might've given me a chance to stand beside other magnificent celestial creatures. That was, until I opened my mouth. Then they would realize their grave mistake and send me back to the earth faster than an angel could lose their wings.

I contemplated how Joe had acted around Sully after the arena breakout. "Are you in some kind of supervisory role with Sully?"

Between him and Sully, I would've picked Sully as the one with more sensibility and the angel better qualified to lead. Because Joe wasn't one to lead by example. If so, we were all in a heap of trouble.

"Fine, you want the full scoop? Well, here it is. I'm an earth angel. I'm assigned to the oversight of fallen angels, like Sully. I also like to keep close to the portal, which Burton oversees," he said as he exchanged one pair of scissors for another from his station.

"The *what*?"

"Burton regulates the traffic to the underworld and manages the gate," Joe said. "Mostly to keep those who have to stay where they belong."

I'd had my suspicions, but it was a little scary hearing Joe put Burton's job into words. "Good to know he's, um... keeping them in."

Joe nodded.

I was relieved that he didn't elaborate further. This was more than enough information for one week. "So, it's over? The nacho cheese spell stuff?"

"No." He drew out the word. "You still have to go

to trial for that with the SHL. Not that it's a real trial or courtroom. They just try to act like it is. Bunch of supernatural buffoons blowing hot air."

I always knew that Joe knew things, but I'd had no idea to what extent. Luckily for me, his lips must've been feeling loose, as he started to spill the beans without me having to pry information out of him. Although, once he started, I wasn't sure I wanted to know the answers.

Turns out, I didn't.

He huffed a sigh. "I knew if I sent you into a place where magic was strictly forbidden that you'd find a way to mess it up. I like to call it the Marissa Factor. If there's trouble, you're bound to find it. I figured Sully was going to need to rescue you. Girl, you need a strong man to keep you in line. I had no idea you'd find a way to drag Grace into your mess. But, hey, it worked out. Maybe the upstairs will take notice and give me a raise if it all goes as planned. Except for the part where you lost my hat. I should've thought that through before lending it to you."

"Wait, you set me up?" I tried to turn to face him but his grip on my hair held me in place. "Then seriously, all you're worried about is that stupid hat? If you're an angel, can't you find a way to get the hat back yourself? Why would you care?"

"I had to throw a fit about the hat because I

wanted to have another reason to send you back to the arena. Although I did love that hat, and you really did need it that day. Losing it wasn't part of the plan. Can't say I know everything, but I sure know enough." He shrugged and kept his focus on my hair.

"Although that's probably why I was assigned to Sully. You..." He shook his head. "Girl, you're harder to guide than a blind man climbing up a magic bean stock—and it's just as hard to gain your trust. Well, you made it an even stickier situation, but that's okay. I like a challenge. I took you on, didn't I?"

"So, why a hairdresser?" It seemed an angel could be all sorts of things, and hairdressing would be low on the list of in-demand jobs.

"Why in the pearly gates not? It's not like I hear people complaining. Would you rather I be a firefighter or some other manly, people-saving job?" He grew wistful and hugged himself. "Mmm, not that there is anything wrong with firefighters. Especially those calendars they used to put out." He snapped his fingers, as if pulling himself out of his own daydream. "But I have my own kind of life-saving calling. Like rescuing witches from horrendous hairdos and earning your eternal gratitude. What would you do without me?"

Joe paused and met my gaze. He knew I wasn't buying it, and he became uncharacteristically serious. "We can all hide our supernatural nature well except for witches. My goal is to help make witches—the good ones, that is—more accepted into society. Witches are the next step up from a mortal, and they shouldn't be judged for that."

I smiled, glad that Joe was my friend. He sure made life more interesting, and it couldn't hurt to have an angel on my side.

"Besides, I like to do hair. I excel at it, and these ladies make my real job easy. No extra surveillance is necessary when they eagerly bring me all the details." He raised his hands to encompass the salon. "Girl, a hair salon is the best place to find out everything about everybody at any time with no effort. It's gossip central."

I grinned, but it faded when a terrible thought struck me. Once Sully was back on track and didn't need Joe's guidance, would Joe leave?

Joe met my terrified stare in the mirror. The tiny bit of color I'd had before was now faded from my face.

"You wouldn't leave me, right, Joe? I'd have to shave my head to avoid everyone seeing every botched spell I've done." I joked to cover my true concern which wasn't about losing a hairdresser, it was about losing a friend.

Joe raised a brow and ran a hand over his smooth, shiny noggin. "What's wrong with bald?"

"Bald isn't a good look for me." I liked to cover my ears. They were a little pointed at the tip, and a few times, I'd been asked if I had elven blood. Not that there was anything wrong with that, but I was one-hundred percent witch and proud of it.

Once Joe busied himself with my hair again, I realized there was a question that he might be able to give me the answer to. Something only he could. "Joe? You said Sully is a fallen angel. What did he do that caused his fall?"

Joe's hands stilled. "I'm not the angel you should be asking."

"You know he won't tell me, and I'd like to know. Not for me, but so I can help him." I met his gaze.

Joe studied me for a long beat until he came to a decision. "All right. I'll tell you. Because you might be the only one who can help with the emotional aspect of the situation." He said the word *emotional* with some distaste. "Goddess knows I can get him to work through all the physical tests, but I can't do anything about his emotional healing. He needs to do that on his own—or perhaps with your help."

I nodded. "I want to help."

To help someone and expect nothing in return. In fact, what I might get in return was a big fat nothing

—no more Sully. Maybe no more Joe. Because once Sully's probation, or whatever it was called, was finished, they would probably both leave me.

"It's not what he did. It's more what he didn't do." Joe shook his head and clucked his tongue. "They're real sticklers upstairs about the rules. You think the military lays down the orders hard, you ought to be working for my boss. No exceptions. Why do you think there are so many demons? Their boss is much more lenient and encourages creativity. Mine... Well, only a select few can handle the responsibility, and even fewer last long enough to be promoted to my role of probation officer."

Joe's backstory was interesting since I didn't know much about how it all worked, but hearing him talk made it sound more like he was fishing for a compliment. When I caught his pointed look as he stared at me in silence, it confirmed my suspicion. "You must be very good at your job."

I could put conviction in the words since he was awesome at hair. The whole angel thing, well, I didn't know how he managed that, but I wasn't one to question. Plus, he had tons of utensils and who-knew-what kind of goop in close proximity to my hair at the moment. This wasn't the time to tick him off.

"So, how long have you been working with Sully on his probation?"

Joe cupped his chin in his palm and drummed his fingers a few times as he considered the question. "Oh, a few hundred years or so. Give or take."

"A few hundred years?" I gaped.

"What? Did I stutter? That's what I said." Joe clucked his tongue again. "That's the thing about a lot of angels. They're so stuck on being do-gooders that when one little thing goes wrong, they have a terrible time getting over it and forgiving themselves. Heck, they punish themselves, so it's not like they need penance for the minor things. Sully actually asked for his punishment."

"He asked to fall? To get kicked out of heaven?" Maybe I'd found someone who was more messed up than me. "That's crazy."

"I told you. They're sticklers," Joe said with a shrug.

"What about you?"

"Oh, honey, I'm nothing like them." He ran his palm over his smooth head. "Heck, I'm nothing like anybody, or anything else. You ought to know that by now."

"It seems like there's a fine line between heaven and hell, and you're walking it half the time," I said.

Joe threw back his head and laughed. "I love a girl who's never afraid to speak her mind." He winked. "So, let me give you the Cliff Notes of why Sully fell, and he can choose to share more details if he ever opens up about it." He rolled his eyes and let one of my curls spring back to my head. "Sully wronged a witch many, many years ago. He found out later that what he thought was doing good actually harmed an innocent, who happened to be a witch. So since then, he's wanted nothing to do with witches."

I grimaced. Again with the dislike of witches? "One bad apple ..." I muttered, not sure if I was referring to the witch, or Sully for his bias.

"It's not because he doesn't like witches, but it's because he's burdened by guilt about what he did, despite it being so long ago. I thought that I'd help along the situation—because seriously, it's been years, hundreds of them—in which Sully saves a witch and it would be the last step in his healing and redemption. Then he could regain his faith in himself, and his wings." Joe held up his hands. "See, it should've been easy-peasy."

I frowned. "Wait a minute. I'm the witch, right?"

Joe shrugged. "Got me."

"When will people ever learn that you can't use others like pawns to try and create a particular outcome? Unlike pawns, when you put a bunch of people together, there's bound to be independent thinking. Whether they're mortal or paranormal doesn't matter; that's the one area where we're all the same," I said.

"You mean how you're stubborn and veering from the path of least resistance to make everything more difficult than it has to be?" Joe smirked. "I tried to fix it so that Sully would have to rescue you, but instead Grace ends up in the slammer. Variable should be your middle name."

"I have to get to work. Can I come back after my shift so you can finish?" When Joe hesitated, I added, "I think you owe me a little since you kind of used me."

He rolled his eyes. "Who got you out of the situation?"

"Fair enough, but really, I'm going to be late for work," I said with another glance at the clock.

"Sure, come back after." Joe started putting his products away.

I stood from the chair. "What you're saying is that if Sully rescues a witch, then he goes back to heaven or to do whatever it is that angels do?"

"Pretty much."

I studied my face in the mirror.

Joe had to have seen my expression fall.

Helping Sully meant saying goodbye. Was I ready to do that?

Walking from Super Strands to the club gave me time to think about all that Joe had said—and all that he hadn't— and to pick up Jasper.

"Don't expect me to keep sneaking you in here." I tucked him into the cubby under the bar, where I'd stashed a few dishtowels to make a little bed.

"I hate staying at the condo while that cat is there." Jasper practically spat the words out. "If Gran were here, she never would've made me share everything. First with Mulder, and now Savvy. It's too much. I need some peace and quiet."

"Well, you've come to the wrong place for that."

I didn't think that was his real reason for wanting to come. Jasper was tongue-tied around Ava's cat. It might've been a love connection if Savvy hadn't walked in on him in the litter box. I didn't think he'd ever recover from the embarrassment.

On the walk over, I'd told Jasper what Joe had shared with me. Despite Jasper's irritable attitude, he was a great listener when he wanted to be.

"Joe always talks in riddles, so I never know if I'm getting the full story," I said. "From my observations, as a demon, Burton doesn't lie. It's not that he means to hurt me. Not having a soul probably means he doesn't have the capacity to worry about such petty things as feelings. Perhaps an angel can't either, but instead avoid telling the whole truth?"

"Riddle me this, riddle me that; why didn't you start by asking the cat?" Jasper tilted his head from side to side.

"That's why."

I turned to shut the cabinet door but stopped when Jasper shouted, "Wait a minute! Let's talk this out."

I paused and turned to him. "You're just stalling to keep me from shutting you in."

"Yes, but still. You know how Joe is. Even before you knew he was angel. He never gives you all the information, and he's surely not going to help you make this decision now. Does he really want you to help Sully?"

I stood. "You have a point."

Was this another test by throwing in what Joe called the Marissa Factor?

I startled when I turned and almost ran smack into Burton. I stood to block the cabinet, although, most likely, he'd already gotten an eyeful of Jasper, or at least detected his scent. He'd never said anything before, but I hated to keep feeling indebted to a demon to keep my secret, friend or not.

"You've been hanging out with that hockey player a lot."

Burton delivered the statement in his usual deadpan manner, but a slight flicker in his eyes told me this was more than an observation. He had a motive somewhere in that head of his in breaking the silence and stating the obvious.

"Yes."

I studied Burton. He didn't initiate conversations. He usually just fielded my babble and rarely responded. Yet here he was waiting for more information.

Something was up, but I didn't know what he was searching for.

"You know Sully's an angel. A fallen one." A slight rising of the corner of his lip displayed either happiness or disdain. With Burton it was hard to tell.

"That doesn't matter." I crossed my arms over my chest, feeling defensive of Sully. Burton still studied me as if he had more to say, but he'd already spoken more than he usually did in a week, so whatever it was, it must've been mighty uncomfortable and probably important.

"It matters to me ... and others."

His cryptic response sent a shiver up my spine. It was the first time I'd ever felt uneasy around Burton; he reminded me of what he was without doing or saying a thing. It was something about the deadness in his eyes. Usually, I never gave his flat features a second glance, but now that he'd shown the slightest alteration in his expression, it only emphasized how dead inside he was.

"What do you want with Sully?" I acted as if it was an idle question, but it erupted a tiny spark of fear in my belly.

The fear wasn't for me. My concern was for Sully.

Burton was never interested in anything, or anyone, unless they served his purpose. He might bartend and bounce at Night Moves, but that wasn't his true purpose; Burton's real job was with the underworld.

And the people who willingly sought out Burton?

I figured that was their problem. A poor choice, sure, but their problem.

Burton inhaled and locked his gaze on me. From

the intensity of his expression, I swore that he'd detected the scent of my fear.

"Don't worry. He'll be the one to decide. He shows much potential." Burton's smile was predatory. He was confiding in me the same way he might share with a coworker or friend about a potential job applicant.

"Potential for what?" I had some ideas, but none of them sounded like anything I wanted to hear.

"So much."

"No offense, Burton, but I don't think Sully wants anything to do with the underworld or consorting with demons."

"But maybe you do," he said.

"What's that supposed to mean?"

I recalled Gloria's comment about Burton, and how she'd left me with a choice. What choice had Gloria made?

"If your hockey boy decides to stay and play, he doesn't have to leave."

I frowned. "Leave? You mean he can keep playing hockey?"

He nodded. "And he doesn't have to leave you."

Burton locked his gaze with mine. He knew the unease that lurked inside, and it wasn't just for Sully. It was about me losing Sully when he regained his rightful place and his wings—leaving just as I started to think there might be something special brewing between us.

I SETTLED IN THE CHAIR AFTER THE LONG SHIFT. Nothing soothed my worries better than getting my hair coiffed to perfection by Joe.

Except for today.

The wash that usually put me nearly to sleep felt rough and uncomfortable, and even Joe's sarcastic banter didn't dispel my fears and doubts.

Jasper curled up in the corner while he waited. Joe glanced at the cat occasionally. Most likely, he suspected Jasper was more than just my cat, but I'd never shared that we could communicate.

Joe dropped a long lock of my hair, and it sprang back into the coil he was battling to dispel. "What is going on with you today?" He put his hands on his narrow hips and cocked his head.

"Nothing."

"What? There's never nothing going on with you. It's always something, even if it's nothing, because you make it into *something*. Plus, I threw out several comments and you didn't come close to taking the bait. Heck, girl, I don't think you even heard me. Now that's a first. So, spill it."

"I don't want to talk about it."

I'd already overstepped my bounds by discussing Sully with Burton. I didn't know what was going on in the whole angels and demons thing, but I didn't want anything to do with it. This wasn't my battle, or my decision. I had to stop making things about me and think about what Sully wanted, and only he knew that.

"Well then, I guess you don't mind having your hair left like this." Joe tilted his head and gestured to the mirror. I met my own distressed gaze and then took in the chaotic state of my hair.

No secret was worth having to leave the salon in this state. I'd be a laughingstock.

Heck, the bum who stole Joe's hat had a better hairstyle than this.

This, even Ava couldn't fix.

Besides, it wasn't really a secret. Joe knew the game. He knew what Burton was and what Sully was striving for. He said his job was to wait on the sidelines, but who was to say a little insider information wouldn't be beneficial? It wasn't like I was spilling a secret.

"Burton is interested in Sully," I said.

"And?"

"What do you mean, *and?* You know what Burton is, and he's never interested in anything. If he's interested in Sully, it can't be good. Plus, I can't say anything to Sully since it would be interfering. He doesn't like it when I interfere. Darn stubborn angel. No offense, Joe."

"Of course, Burton is interested in Sully, and you don't have to tell the boy; he already knows. Everybody with an ounce of celestial blood knows that. Just what do you think Burton is?" Thankfully, Joe resumed working on the explosion of frizz and curls that was my hair as he waited for my response.

"How many times are you going to ask me that? He's a demon." Even though the others in the salon could easily overhear with their supernatural hearing, I whispered the words.

"You don't have to worry about anyone in here eavesdropping. They don't give bat on a cracker about our conversation. But if it makes you feel better, I'll turn up the tunes." He jerked his head and the eighties music increased in volume. "Even if it doesn't make you feel better, it *does* make me feel better." He smiled with pleasure at the annoyed glances of the other customers.

"What do you think Burton was before he was a demon?" Joe asked. "Why do you think he has the position he does? Not every demon gets to be a recruiter. He probably wouldn't admit to that role."

"I don't know."

Demons didn't start as demons? Until now, I didn't know Burton was a recruiter; I thought people sought him out on their own. I was beginning to feel as if I'd lived most of my life in a bubble. Surely, I couldn't be *that* clueless about everything in this supernatural world.

"There's a whole lot of inbreeding in that pool, if you ask me. But you didn't ask me. Some started out as other paranormal entities and got recruited, but high-ranking ones like Burton—they started off as angels. Why do you think we can detect each other when no one else can?"

"Burton was an angel?" I couldn't have been more surprised if Joe had told me that he was giving up hairspray as his New Year's resolution. "That's not possible."

I'd finally accepted Joe's angelic heritage, but that had taken some work until I realized he had his own quirky way of doing things but was generally a nice guy.

I might like Burton, but being a nice guy was never something I'd accuse him of.

"That's what losing your soul will do to you. Once you accept that you've fallen from grace and either can't be reformed or decide you don't want to reform, you're recruited for the underworld. It's one way or the other; there's no grey area," he said as he ran a brush through my hair.

"Of course, there's no grey area, why would there be?" More rules. I was sick of rules. Another thought tickled the back of my mind. I didn't want to say it, because it was a terrible thought to have, but like Burton, Joe probably already knew what I was thinking. "If Sully chooses Burton, that means he'll get to stay?"

Joe raised a brow and nodded. "Um ... *hmm*." He made a clucking sound in the back of his throat. "Oh, if he does, I can't wait to see the fireworks from your sister. Imagine what she'll think about you having a demon as your boyfriend."

"He's not my boyfriend." Yet. I hadn't thought about Ava. I think part of her was secretly happy that I was showing interest in an angel, fallen or not. But this wasn't about me; this was about Sully. "How much time does he have?"

Joe shrugged. "That's not for me to say."

"Of course, it's not." Joe could say it; I knew he was lying. He just wasn't going to. "It's because Sully isn't allowed to know, right?"

Joe's shift in expression told me I'd hit the nail on the head—or the angel on his halo. "But I'm not Sully; you can tell me. I'll keep it a secret."

Joe laughed harder than I'd ever seen him laugh

before. He bent over and clutched his knees, chortling in a very un-angel like manner until his eyes watered enough to smear the liner surrounding them.

"*You?* Keep a secret? That's the most ridiculous thing I ever heard. Girl, you spilled your guts because you were concerned about your hair, so I don't think you'd be able to keep something a little more stressful, like choosing between heaven and hell, under wraps. No, I think I'll pass on sharing this, Sully will have to figure it all out on his own. That's what he wants anyway, isn't it? Besides, don't you have a trial coming up to worry about? Seems like you have enough of your own problems."

Joe resumed working on my hair, stopping every few minutes to laugh again and mutter about my leaky lips, or other slang referring to my chatter. Sully did want to figure things out on his own, so who was I to interfere?

Just a lowly, talkative witch, with horrendous, uncontrollable hair and the inability to spell my way out of a jam, who happened to be interested in a fallen angel.

❧ 16 ❧

Patience was never my strong point.

By the next morning, I had decided to take matters into my own hands. I felt a little guilty eavesdropping, but I had to know what was in store for Sully.

"I don't think this is a good idea." Jasper paused from cleaning his paw.

"You never think any of my charms or potions are a good idea," I said.

"Because they usually aren't." He turned in a circle and curled up on my bed.

"Just think, if I hadn't messed up the charmed cocktail that one time, we wouldn't be having this conversation." I winked at Jasper and dropped the remaining ingredients into the cauldron. A wave of my hand over the top caused smoke to rise and gather in a small cloud on the ceiling.

"Angels have secrets and a few I must know.

Allow me to listen to Sully and Joe."

A pinpoint of light opened in the middle of the ceiling and grew until an image wavered. I laid on the bed and closed my eyes to view the scene in my mind. The items in the room I viewed shifted and settled.

The salon was empty except for Joe. He was putting away the last of his items at his station. After closing the drawer, he froze and lifted his head, as if listening.

I tensed and pulled back from the image. Could he sense my presence?

Before I could fret further or disable the spell, Sully walked into the salon.

"Hello, Joesephoria. It's been a while."

"I go by Joe here. And you knew we'd run into each other again eventually. I've been waiting for you to come to me." Joe folded his arms and leaned against the counter, raising a brow as he ran his gaze over Sully.

Sully scowled. "For your help?"

"No, I wouldn't expect you to ask for help or accept it. You're stubborn that way. But eventually, you'd need to make a decision, and I suspected this one was going to be a little more difficult than you had imagined."

Sully nodded and averted his gaze. "I didn't consider the consequences."

"*You never do. That's what makes you a good angel, but a bad boyfriend. You want to stay with her, don't you?*"

I held my breath, waiting for Sully's response, but uncertain of what I wanted him to say. For a moment, he seemed to stare out of the image and into my eyes.

He straightened as if shouldering a burden. "What I want and what I do are two different things. My needs are never first. They shouldn't be. Not if I want to wear these wings like they're supposed to be worn. Service and sacrifice. That's what I signed up for."

"*But you weren't expecting to care for her, were you?*"

"*No. But I assume most people don't expect it. Joe, how can I hurt her like this?*"

"*She's tougher than you give her credit for. If that is your decision, she'll learn to live with it. Are you prepared to live with that?*"

"*Do I have a choice?*"

"*There's always a choice.*" *Joe hesitated and then said,* "*Have you spoken to Burton?*"

"*You mean the very direct demon? He sure doesn't worry about beating around the bush. He gets right to the point and probably wouldn't hesitate to put it right through my heart if it served him.*"

Joe laughed and waived his hand at Sully. "*It wouldn't. Provoking you like that would result in an angry fallen angel. That wouldn't serve his purposes. You'd spend eternity looking for a way to retaliate. He wants you of your own free will, and he knows he has the key to open your heart."*

"Marissa."

Joe nodded. "Don't you find it ironic that she happens to be a witch?"

"I thought that was kind of a cruel twist."

"Of fate?"

"I don't believe in fate."

"You should. It's what most of the world is built on. Kind of what makes it go around. Without it, we might do whatever we please, and you know what that leads to."

"More clientele for Burton?"

"Yes, but more importantly, more for me. Imagine how many jealous and angry streaks I'd be cleaning up? I'd be booked from now until infinity."

Sully looked around the salon as if seeing it for the first time. "You never said why you chose to work as a hairdresser."

"You never asked." Joe shrugged. "It comes naturally. Perhaps like you and your hockey. Sure, my angel dust goes a long way repairing that which is otherwise irreparable. Plus, I get to be privy to all the gossip and know where to focus my attention. So, yes, there's a method to my madness."

I opened my eyes and released myself from the listening spell.

I knew it! Joe was using magic with my hair.

I also knew his full name. Not that I'd ever use it. Names had power, which was why many paranormal didn't share their real—or full—name. That was why Sully wielded that little nugget of information over Joe.

Sully didn't want my help; still, somehow, I was going to give it to him by letting him know he could go if he needed to. But I wouldn't force his hand to make a decision. It might be difficult for me to do, but it was about time I started cleaning up my karma and do something for someone else.

⚜

I couldn't believe my luck.

There he sat—the bum I'd seen on television. Back on the same corner, with his pile of stuff. Joe's autographed hat was perched on top of another knitted cap on his head. The hat looked stained and more worse for wear, but Joe might be happy to have it back instead of the new hat I'd picked up at the arena.

Now I could use the new one to barter to get the old one back.

I stopped in front of the man. His head hung forward, and I wondered if he'd fallen asleep. I could've grabbed the hat and made a run for it, but I wasn't the kind of witch to take advantage of someone so obviously disadvantaged.

I cleared my throat and waited until he lifted his head, and then dug for some coins in the bottom of my purse. After dropping the change in the paper cup, I smiled.

"Hello." I put my hand on my cocked hip. "That's a cool hat."

The bum reached for Joe's hat and gripped the bill. He must've detected my eagerness to have his hat. "Mine."

"I know, but it looks kind of old." And dirty as heck. If I did get it back, Joe was going to kill me, or at least give me the worst haircuts for several months. "I could get you a newer, better one." I reached in my purse and pulled out one of the new Sully hat trick hats.

He bent forward to squint at the hat and then shook his head, returning to recline against the building. "Nope. Mine is autographed."

I frowned and tucked the new hat behind me. I hadn't thought about that. Joe would probably have the same complaint.

Might as well fix that now.

"So is this one." I mumbled a spell under my

breath and then held the hat forward again for his inspection, hoping I'd said the spell loud enough for it to work.

It had.

"That ain't Sully's signature," the bum said.

"Yes, it is." I shook the hat, which clearly displayed the autograph of Sullivan Sexton. I'd even added in a cute little number 69 beside it, just to make it more convincing.

"That ain't how he signs his name. He signs it 'Sully' and never signs his full name. Everybody knows that. You got yourself a fake. Or maybe it's 'cause you put that little spell on it hoping I wouldn't notice." His grin displayed his few remaining teeth.

He straightened and tucked Joe's coveted hat into one of his garbage bags filled with his possessions and goddess knows what else that were stacked beside him. "Don't think because I'm living on the street that I'm stupid. Or that I don't know a witch when I see one. Or that I don't know the value of this hat you're trying to get from me with this fake one you're trying to pass off."

Of all the bums on the street, I had to get one that actually knew hockey and had an attitude against witches. "He signed it ..."

The bum crossed his arms.

I sighed and turned away.

This wasn't worth the effort. If I got the hat back, it was going to smell from residing within all the bum's crap, and Joe probably wouldn't want it anyway. "I should've kept my change."

"You is a greedy witch too," he called after me.

If this dude knew the hat had a fake signature, no way would I be able to convince Joe it was legit.

I left empty-handed and continued to the arena. With Grace freed, there weren't many witches left picketing. I doubted I'd get the same support for my trial as Grace had.

Since I couldn't get in, I waited near the player's entrance until I saw Sully approach for his early skating practice. "Listen. I know what you are."

Sully tensed and stepped away. "No, you don't."

I waved him off. "You don't have to hide from me."

"Wings don't mean anything. What's on the outside doesn't define who you are on the inside," he said.

"Exactly."

Pain flitted across his face. "I've fallen. I'm only a few steps away from being a demon."

I could've told him I knew at least one demon that wasn't too bad, but I didn't think that would make him feel any better. "You're still an angel.

Anything you did before can't change who, or what, you are now. Believe me, if that were so, the witches might've taken my witch card back a long time ago."

I hesitated. "So, if that's a thing—taking back my witch status or magic—maybe don't mention that. It might give them ideas." Some witches would happily strip me of my magic faster than Lee could fling an insult.

Sully settled on the edge of a bench and hung his head. "The hockey helps me work through my anger. The physical work is good, and the skating... Well, it's the closest I can get to flying."

"Is it uncomfortable to have to keep your wings tucked away?"

He shrugged. "Not always. I need to stretch them now and then like any other part of my body kept immobile for too long." He paused. "As a mortal, I wasn't good at much of anything except hockey. As an angel, I messed that up, too. I was supposed to lie low within the melting pot of mortals and paranormal, not become an overnight hockey superstar. Now the past that was carefully crafted to hide my true origins is at risk of exposing me for what I really am."

"I'm sorry," I said, and I meant it. "I was only trying to get rid of a nacho cheese stain on Grace's jersey. I didn't mean to spell you."

He furrowed his brow. "Spell me? As an angel, I'm impervious to a spell."

I blinked. "Why didn't you say that?" If he had, then it would've eliminated the entire mess with Grace and the guilt I'd been carrying, but it would've also exposed him as an angel. But he had denied it immediately and said Grace was innocent.

I sighed. "I guess I understand why you didn't say anything."

It made sense now how he seemed to appear on the hockey scene out of nowhere. If he regained his angel status, his brief hockey career would be over. He'd have to either quit, retire, get injured, or fall off the face of the earth—literally.

I sat and placed my hand on his shoulder. When he didn't flinch, I moved closer and touched the tip of his wing concealed beneath his shirt. Despite my questionable antics, my nefarious friends, and my inability to adhere to most rules, I coveted the glorious wings. No wonder so many mortals were desperate to be included into the fold. "How have you kept these hidden?"

"Once they're fully open, they're not visible to most, and most only see their shadow," he said while avoiding my gaze.

The reality of his heritage slowly sunk in. *He was*

an angel. It was official—any thoughts I'd had of any more than a friendship with Sully were squelched. He was way too good for me. "I'm sorry. For whatever happened that makes you feel this way."

He turned to me, and I gazed into his dark eyes. I wanted to take away the pain swirling around the little gems of light in his eyes. Peering into their depths made me feel that there was hope for any situation.

He hung his head. "Living with the shame is the hardest. I know I was tricked, but I shouldn't have been. My job was to sort the fact from the fiction. Weakness allowed my heart to misguide me, and I learned too late that I'd used my greatest gifts for evil."

"You didn't know," I said.

"I should have."

Arguing about his guilt was fruitless. I'd carried that burden around myself too many times and always refused to put it down until I was ready. He would have to be the one to release the guilt.

"Her name was Sarah."

I caught my breath and waited for him to continue.

"I thought I was helping her, but it turned out I was aiding and abetting her crimes. Imagine that: an angel helping to sell souls. She'd lost her own long ago and thought no one else needed theirs."

Any retort I might have had stuck in my throat. A witch selling souls? This was serious stuff. I didn't know there was a spell to do that.

"Back then, the supernatural community wasn't as open as they are now," he said. "We lived in the shadows. I exposed her for what she was to the mortals. By doing so I might as well have tied the noose around her neck and burnt her body myself. As soon as the word was out, her days were numbered, and no place was safe. The paranormals kept their distance. They feared they'd be taken in on the grounds of being guilty by association. If that happened, the stealthy life they'd been able to live up till that point would've been challenged."

I put my hand on his arm, knowing there wasn't anything I could say.

Sully sighed. "It was wrong for me to do it. I took pleasure in her downfall. But since then, I've suffered every day. First because of the angels, since I'd exposed the supernatural community and put others at risk. She was wrong for what she did, but they'd wanted to handle it, and I didn't follow the chain of command. I signed and sealed her fate without a thought of the consequences for me or anyone else that had been put in danger."

"But based on her actions, she wasn't innocent." Not innocent, but a witch. If other witches—especially Ava—knew what Sully had done, they'd be furious.

"It wasn't my place to make that decision. I didn't have the right to judge her," he said.

As a cocktail waitress, I'd lent an ear to many over the years, but a fallen angel? No one would believe that one. They'd be more likely to nod and agree that it made sense that a demented demon or one of Satan's underlings would come knocking at my door, but not an angel.

"Thank you for listening." He tentatively placed his hands on my shoulders and met my gaze. "I'm no angel."

I tilted my head back. "Neither am I."

He slid his hands upward until he cupped my face and bent toward me. The kiss was soft and inquisitive.

I pulled away. "Is a kiss going to be a problem for you to... you know, regain your angel status?"

If he said yes, could I convince him to maintain his righteous path? I couldn't be the one responsible for the denial of his readmission.

"No. Most angels start out as mortals. We might have lost a lot of things that come with that package, but this isn't one of them," he smiled.

Gold speckles of light reflected in his eyes, mesmerizing me. I might've thought my intoxication was due to some angel trick if I wasn't so utterly charmed.

❧ 17 ❧

I snuggled into the couch and tried to encourage Mulder to join me. The rambunctious furball wanted nothing to do with rest and relaxation. He probably slept the entire time I went out and assumed I returned home to entertain him.

The dog raced around the room in a circle, the long hair on his tail trailing behind him.

Unfortunately, his mindless and clueless pursuit of everything and nothing reminded me all too much of myself. The way he stumbled through life with a sappy smile on his face, oblivious to the potential danger of Savvy watching him nearby, who was ready to give him a swat if he got too close.

I consorted with demons—well, one demon. Surely an angel wasn't going to want anything to do with me once he realized my limited circle and a few unsavory friends. That would be unlikely.

So far, he hadn't mentioned working as a fallen angel with Burton. Could he live with that?

From my limited experience with what Burton did, it seemed his type served a purpose for those who'd grown tired of the time and trouble required to meet their goals. Even with the help of magic, and supernatural abilities, some people were always looking over that mountain for the easiest way to climb it.

"He's better off with someone like you." I didn't have to tell Ava who I was talking about. Fallen or not, Sully was a better person than I was on my best day.

"I don't think so." She sat beside me and waited for me to elaborate. She knew all she had to do was open the door to the conversation and be my sounding board. She was awesome like that.

"Why, nothing for you to fix?" I teased. "I suppose it would be kind of hard to lecture an angel."

I might love to root for the underdog and embrace their uniqueness, but Ava tried to fix them.

"I don't lecture people," she protested with little conviction.

There was no way she could convince me other-wise. What she considered pointing out the obvious risks and rewards of most situations, I considered a boring lecture on how to sit back and watch the rest of the world live.

Ava stood. "Right now, we need to wrap up this bogus trial. I call this an opportunity to reduce discrimination against witches."

Ava always was a big picture kind of gal, while I thrived on immediate gratification and often couldn't see farther than the tip of my nose.

"Let's get this over with," I said, ready to face the SHL.

THE ROOM WAS NOTHING LIKE WHAT I HAD envisioned a courtroom would look like, but Ava fit the image of every lawyer I'd seen on television. She had watched those shows obsessively while we were growing up.

I stopped to hug Grace on my way to the front. "How are you doing?"

Grace had been released with a weak apology and free tickets for the hockey season once I had confessed to casting the arena spell. The issue now was proving it had been a mistake, a no-harm-no-foul kind of spell, and certainly one that couldn't have impacted Sully's skills.

"I'm fine," she said.

"Brian?" I hoped to confirm the rumor that he'd broken off their relationship when Grace needed him most wasn't true.

Grace waved her hand. "No big loss. At least he showed his true colors now before things got serious."

I leaned in to whisper, "Do you want me to mix a potion for him?"

Grace embraced me and laughed. "I'm not that mad at him," she said. "Now go get to your seat to get this joke over with."

I settled into the hard, wooden bench to wait for the trial to start. Considering that the so-called trial was at the hockey arena in one of their many rooms tucked away, the whole weird situation stunk of bad magic, especially when Gloria walked in.

Grace tracked her progress down the aisle with a narrowed gaze.

Gloria had never bothered to hide her true nature. Her ebony hair hung to her waist and glistened under the dim lighting when it caught on her locks. She settled into the chair between the two men overseeing the proceedings. The worst part was confirming that she was part owner of the hockey arena. It made the restrictions on magic and witches seem much more personal.

Jealousy and spite could fuel a lot of little fires.

Ava stepped up to the desk where the three people sat to act as both judge and jury for my indiscretion. I couldn't refer to it as a crime. Magic wasn't illegal, and my spell wasn't intentional, so the only crime I'd committed in their eyes was my inability to comprehend hockey's endless rules.

A quick glance behind me confirmed what I'd suspected.

Lee sat in with the small gathering of spectators. Most likely, he'd be called to testify since I had worked with him briefly, though he'd probably have been here regardless just to see me get dissected.

Although he hadn't counted on me coming with an ally in the likes of Joe. Lee's eyes had widened when he first saw Joe, and he'd scuttled his skinny little butt to the end of the aisle to put some distance between Joe's glare and himself.

Good thing I didn't have the need to call Burton in for this, or Lee might spontaneously combust on the spot.

Sometimes it helped to have friends in low places.

When Ava cleared her throat, I returned my attention to the front of the room.

"We're here today for these ridiculous proceedings to confirm what should be obvious: that Marissa Hale didn't intentionally perform magic, and that this persecution is unethically directed at witches and discriminatory in nature." Ava raised her voice slightly as she finished and spun on her heel to face the crowd.

Gloria stood. "Witches aren't on trial here. Just this witch."

She narrowed her gaze on me, resurrecting the visual of that eye popping out and swimming around in her drink glass. The memory gave me indigestion every time I thought about it.

Ava smiled and spoke without turning towards Gloria. "If witches were on trial for misdeeds, then there is at least one in this room who'd be at the top of that persecution." She ran her hand over her uniform locks to draw the attention to Gloria's blatant disregard for hiding nasty spelling. "I call Marissa's hairstylist to the stand."

Joe stood on his stilettos. "I'll stand, but there really isn't a stand here, is there?" He sashayed to the front of the room. "This," he gestured to the room, "is a complete waste of my valuable time. Do you have any idea how much I make an hour doing hair? Which goes to say that I know the secrets of the most prestigious witches in this community. They come to me to cover up their little indiscretions, and based upon that, I know a thing or two about magic. Such as who can do what and how well, and I can tell you that my girl Marissa has had many a spelling mistake. None were intentional, and none powerful enough to elevate someone's hockey skill level."

The SHL man at the desk with eyebrows rivaling two black caterpillars had the nerve to speak up and interrupt Joe, behavior unheard of from anyone who knew him. "But what about that black streak in her hair?"

My face heated as my lack of spelling skill was put on display. I self-consciously reached up to pat my head. I thought I'd concealed the telling locks, but they must have pulled loose. Sometimes it was as if the ill-behaved hair had a mind of its own and was attempting to make its own mischief.

Joe rolled his eyes. "*That* has been there for years. I've tried to get rid of it, but to no avail. Sometimes those can be tricky. But it wasn't from a hockey spell. It wasn't from that little dance—which I might add was more awesome than anything that bumbling beer bozo could ever do. That, my disillusioned friend, was for spilled nacho cheese."

This might have been the only time I should be happy about my inadequacies. This whole mess had taken the wind from Sully's sails and the enjoyment from his hockey glory. I needed to clear his name and make it known that his skill was his doing and not from a spell. He was magic on the ice all on his own.

The man frowned. "Then what was it for? To have a streak that resistant to change must've been the result of a terrible spell."

Ava spoke up. "That goes to show you how much you know about witches. Yet, you place these rules and restrictions upon them. One way to get a black streak is by becoming frightened while completing a spell. Marissa, would you care to elaborate?"

My face burned like a furnace because *no, I didn't want to elaborate*. Ava knew that, which was why she left it up to me to determine if I wanted to share the truth, or at least make the reason behind the streak seem a little more substantial.

But this was for Sully, so I lifted my head.

The black streak had been there before Jasper; it had only gotten bigger after I gained my furry side-kick. Then it had grown more once I'd spilled the nacho cheese.

I might as well start from the beginning. "I was stirring a medicinal spell when I was startled by a spider."

"A spider? Who is she, Little Miss Muffet?" One of the judges said with a laugh.

Laughter erupted in the makeshift courtroom.

Ava straightened. "No, she's a good witch."

"So you say! I know all about her medicinal spells. She uses them while working at Night Moves to make witches ill so she can snag their appointments with that hairdresser." Gloria pointed her long fingernail at Joe.

Joe spun on his heel and waved his hand at Gloria. "She doesn't need to do that to get an appointment with me. We're friends." His words made it obvious that Gloria was not on his list of friends.

Joe was lying to try to get me out of this mess. I'd had enough lies. "Gloria's right. I have done that. But that's my worst crime when it comes to spelling, and it's not anything that impacts the SHL."

The three men who served as judge and jury whispered amongst themselves until Ava announced, "We have an eyewitness testimony."

I tensed for a moment, fearing that Gloria would pop her fake eye out of its socket to testify against me. At this point, not much would surprise me.

Ava gestured toward the back of the room. "I would like to call Harold Moonsniff."

"Who?" I spun to see the werewolf who had been seated next to me during the game strutting into the room. His frame was so huge he barely made it up the center aisle without knocking over my chair. He settled into a chair as the video footage from the game was played, displaying him sitting beside me.

"There was no way she'd have any reason try to spell the game," the were said. "All she cared about was those darn nachos, and she kept on flapping her gums the entire time and trying to stand up during plays. She was a disgrace as a hockey fan. The only reason she would have to spell the game would be if she wanted it to end quicker so she could leave."

Wow, the big dude sure had formed an opinion about me in a short time.

"Thank you, Harry." Ava stepped to the front of the desk. "One important element is being over-looked, and that is what is really on trial. And that is the rules the SHL has against magic."

The three men behind the desk grumbled until one blurted, "Wait a minute."

"We've determined that this witch," she pointed at Gloria, "is part of the SHL. She is not representa-tive of witches. She was seeking vengeance against your star hockey player for actions against her daughter ages ago, who had crossed the line by trying to do the work of demons. Once exposed, Gloria's daughter went to hell, and Gloria has made it her mission to get her out, no matter what the cost. The witches didn't come to her aid then, so she hasn't wanted anything to do with them since."

My head spun to find Sully, but he was not in the room. The witch he had wronged all those years ago was Gloria's daughter?

"This witch on your payroll wants her daughter

released from her sentence to eternity in hell and wanted to exchange two witches for her daughter." Ava gestured toward Grace and me. "Gloria also knows that getting a witch in trouble on Sully's watch will only exacerbate his guilt over what he did. She doesn't care who gets hurt in the process."

She crossed her arms. "I rest my case."

I turned and met Gloria's gaze. She raised her brows in inquiry. I'd never intended to respond to her offer, because there was no question of my decision. I swiveled to face the front and gave her my back.

If I didn't know better, I might've thought a little sadness showed in her eyes at my rebuff. It made me wonder if she had wanted to make me into the daughter she'd lost. Despite the decades that had passed, she acted as if her wound was still fresh.

I wouldn't feed Gloria's thirst for vengeance with my own anger. After what she did to Grace, which I'd probably always feel responsible for, and what she put Sully through—knowing full well the mental anguish this would cause him—a little spell wouldn't give me enough satisfaction. Instead, I'd give her something she probably never had before and never expected from the likes of me.

I'd give her empathy and understanding.

Gloria stood as if to leave and I said, "It must be unbearably hard to lose a daughter. No matter how much time has passed, I can't imagine how painful that must be."

Gloria stopped in her tracks, and her brows rose. It wasn't what she expected to hear from me. "No, you can't. Stop trying to pacify me or distract me with your false condolences. You don't fool me. You're just like the rest of them. You would have been one of the first ones to burn her at the stake or cast the first stone. You think you're better than everyone else—better than her."

Her angry words echoed through the room as the guards approached.

18

Sometimes fate has a way of intervening in life.

As if Burton knew Sully had approached Joe, he made his move on Sully and pressured him to make a decision.

This time, I didn't even require a listening spell since I stumbled upon them in the employee break room at Night Moves.

We hadn't opened yet, and I hadn't expected to find anyone in there at that hour. Luckily, I'd not alerted them to my presence, so when I heard voices and recognized who they belonged to, I stopped short of the open doorway and struggled to remain silent.

The door was cracked open, and I peered into the room. Perhaps since they were immersed in the conversation, their supernatural sense of hearing and smell wouldn't betray my presence. Although, since I worked here almost every day, I was sure if they did notice, they might not attribute it to my scent, since my stink was probably all over this place.

Burton's deadpan voice floated out into the hall. "You have not yet made a decision. Is the girl not enough to keep you here? Or the superstar status in the sport you enjoy?"

"I didn't ask for your help with any of that, and Marissa isn't a bargaining chip." Sully's voice rose with irritation.

"Who said I would use her to bargain with you? Even I am not stupid enough to try and force the will of a rambunctious witch." Burton's gaze flickered to the door.

Sully cringed as the insult appeared to hit home. "I paid the price for my mistake, but it seems that it will never be forgotten."

Burton shrugged. "Many angels have done much worse. Your biggest mistake was getting caught. The angels used you as an example." Burton pressed on, "It's a job, and you could do it well, while you keep your hockey fame and Marissa, if you choose."

"How can you sell her out like that? She thinks you're her friend," Sully said.

Burton's gaze sought my hiding place again, so I

pulled back and flattened myself against the wall, allowing myself to still hear, but not see, them.

"I'm not selling her out. I'm stating the obvious. Even a fool could see that the girl cares for you, and you her. I am her friend—as much as I can be. I don't know how to have, or be, a friend."

"They take that with your soul, I assume."

Burton shrugged. "Not a big loss. I can't remember how it felt before. Besides, it's easier to make decisions without concerns about right or wrong. If witches could learn that, then perhaps they wouldn't have such a rainbow of colors gracing their hair. I don't see that it matters, but it bothers Marissa. If I could, I would offer her the same deal as you, but I cannot strike that deal with a witch." He paused, as if in reflection. "I guess that is something a friend might do."

The sound of a door closing indicated that Sully hadn't provided him with an answer, let alone a response. I peeked in to confirm that Burton was alone. His back was to me, facing the side door that Sully had exited. I prepared to return to the club and pretend I hadn't overheard them, until Burton's voice made me pause.

"Did I do okay?" Burton didn't turn when he spoke.

I shrugged and realized he hadn't seen my gesture. "You knew I was back here."

"Of course." Burton turned to face me, his expressionless face not revealing one iota of information on how he felt their interaction had gone and what Sully might decide. "Yes, I did know you were there, but figured I would say what I thought anyway."

"You always do." That was one thing I could always count on with Burton. He had absolutely no filter. "Besides, it doesn't matter, it's his decision." I dropped my gaze to the ground.

"It might be his decision, but you will influence it whether you want to or not. It's too late to change that. I hadn't counted on you helping me play my hand. That was convenient."

Even though I had no desire for Sully to give up his wings and not get his grace back, I was curious as to what deal Burton was offering. How difficult was the decision Sully had to make between the likes of Burton and Joe? It would seem as if Joe was the easy, logical decision, but that came with a lot of penance and rules. Burton seemed like he spent most of his life giving the finger to rules and worried more about ... nothing.

"What would Sully do if he agreed to your deal?"

"It's not really a deal. He has already fallen. I'm not

taking away anything that he has. He would just not get it back and would learn to embrace the elements of the earth. As a turned angel, he has a chance of fitting in and forgetting about the righteousness of heaven, except he resists that," Burton said. "One only has to look around the world to see that we already live in a little bit of hell. Going a few steps further isn't really that different, if you look at it that way."

"He'd recruit others, like you do?" Picturing Sully with the flat expression Burton wore day in and day out sent a shudder through me. Despite knowing there was more to Burton beneath the surface even with his emotionless exterior, I hated to think of what Sully would become.

"Not exactly like me. My job is more oversight. The ones you call recruiters send people to me. His role in hockey enables him to be around a lot of people who want many things, but especially fame and fortune. Our job is to help them achieve that. If he went with Joe, then their teachings and rules would tell him that those things are not important. That it is more important to help those in need—the weak, the poor. We believe in the survival of the fittest. The extra effort goes the extra mile, and everyone has things that are important to them, even if they may be frivolous and a little greedy. But what more is there to enjoy in this world if we are not taking advantage of what we can?"

That was the most Burton had ever spoken. His explanation removed all the evil from what he did. He almost made it sound like a good thing, and it was obvious he believed what he said. For a man of few words, he might be an excellent salesperson.

"So, Sully would keep on doing what he's doing?"

Burton stepped away and locked the outside door so no one could sneak into the club once we opened. He must've been expecting Sully since it had been open. "He could do whatever he wants, or I should say, whatever the underworld wants. Except, unlike the other guys, we believe there's nothing wrong with relationships or love." He looked to me.

I didn't know if it was love. With angels and demons involved, it would be hard to determine if someone wasn't using me as a means to the end they desired.

I LEANED ON THE BAR TO STUDY THE IMAGES ON the television set. The hockey game looked different now that I knew one of the players. Although my interest wasn't exactly with the game, but more with concern about the guys chasing him down the ice with sticks with the intent to stop Sully no matter what.

It had been hours since Sully had left the club, and I'd had trouble keeping him off my mind despite how much the club was hopping.

That guy who'd been seeking Burton last week was back again, but wisely avoiding me. He didn't need to bother since I didn't have the energy to deter him this time. If he made the wrong choice now, he couldn't say he wasn't warned.

I cringed when one of the big players slammed another one off the boards. That type of move seemed to be encouraged. Big dudes, usually werewolves or shifters, protected the stars.

It seemed silly to worry about an angel getting hurt. I would think they'd have some ability to heal themselves, but I wasn't sure that applied to a fallen angel. I thought that ability was lost with the whole retaking back the grace thing. That left Sully vulnerable on the ice with a bunch of guys with at least some paranormal blood flowing through their veins. He was practically mortal among them.

"If he chose to stay and play, I assume he'd gain some way to heal himself, to get stronger." I murmured the words.

"Of course. That, and more."

I hadn't expected a response since I hadn't heard

Burton approach, but he had that ability of extreme stealth that had made me initially suspect he was a vamp before learning his true nature.

Burton circled the bar to pick up a glass and began to polish it while watching me watch the television.

Sully crouched and pulled back his stick to strike the puck. I tensed as it sailed above the goalie and in high and to the right. The buzzer sounded, and the light behind the net indicated that he'd hit his mark. Sully did a fist pump and raised his stick to take in the cheers from the crowd as they played a celebratory song.

Burton reached under the bar to ring the goal bell he'd recently installed. He then played a short clip of the song they played at the game when they scored, to incite everyone in the bar to celebrate with the team. This usually resulted in an increased drink order, which made Vlad happy. I'd initially thought that Burton installed this for the love of the game, but recent details told me there was more to it than that.

I looked to Burton. "You want him to be a star, don't you? You think it will help convince him to stay and join your ... team."

"Of course. It's a win for everyone. Vlad is happy because it brings in more business for the club. Sully is happy because he gets to play the game that he loves and is recognized for it. You're happy because he stays."

I frowned.

Sully had been to Night Moves more often recently. This brought other players to the bar and more business. I thought it had started with me, but maybe I'd been wrong all this time.

"Burton, did you have something to do with how well Sully plays now?" One thing I'd found with Burton was that if you asked him a direct question, he told you the truth. I didn't know if it was a demon thing, or the whole lack-of-a-soul thing, or just that he didn't care. I was leaning toward the not caring.

He nodded. "Of course. He stunk at hockey before."

"Before what?"

"When he used to play hockey as a mortal. I only gave him what he always wanted. Sometimes it takes a little visualization to realize all the options that are available if you ask. But he'd never ask. He's too stubborn."

So, Sully was right; there had been some intervention in his amazing skill. But it wasn't divine intervention, and it wasn't magic; it was the demons who wanted him.

That might be worse.

I closed my eyes and sighed. "Burton, you shouldn't have intervened."

"Why? That's my job," he said. "It makes you happy, too. I like to make you happy."

Without the ability to weigh the right and wrong of a situation, it would be impossible to explain to Burton that we didn't always get what we wanted without working for it. That it wasn't the same if it was given to us, and especially if there were strings attached. And with Burton, there were plenty of strings attached.

"The angels don't like for one to have so much focus on their individual satisfaction. What is wrong with that?" As Burton stared at me, imploring me to understand, I considered what he said.

"What do you mean 'you like to make me happy?' This has to do with Sully," I said.

In my mind, the chain of events started with Burton influencing Sully. That night I went to the game and spelled the jersey. From what Burton was saying, there had been no spell interfering with the game. I'd had nothing to do with that, or with Grace's arrest. But I wouldn't have even been to the game if Brian hadn't gotten sick. Sully might've become a star, but he wouldn't have come to the club, met Burton, and learned of the potential to stay.

Joe had implied that he had intervened in some

way to make me go to the game, but with the way he spoke in riddles, I couldn't tell if he was trying to push me to discover the truth or not. "Burton. Did you have something to do with Brian getting sick that night?"

"Of course. I needed you to go to the game. It worked out well, don't you think?"

Would I change that fateful night now, even knowing how it began? It gave Sully the opportunity to really shine doing something he loved, even if it was his fifteen minutes of fame. It let me meet Sully and discover what love could be like.

Grace was out of jail, and Joe... Well, I'd get him another hat. Would I change any of this knowing what lead to it? Even though Burton did have his own interests at heart, he meant to do something nice for me.

"You are happy now. You were sad for so long, and cranky, about men. I don't like dealing with you when you're cranky all the time. It gets tiresome." He stated the facts as if his actions were reasonable.

"You wouldn't have anything to do with how Ava found all that out about Gloria?"

Burton raising his brow slightly was all the answer I needed. He never lied. He had no reason to, but it seemed that a demon was uncomfortable with doing what might be considered a good deed. "Giving one piece of the puzzle isn't solving it."

"What?"

Burton left without clarifying his odd statement that reminded me of Joe.

I looked back to the television where Sully's face was highlighted on the screen as he skated around the ice in a kind of victory lap. Hats rained down from the stands to signify that he'd once again had a hat trick.

Three goals in a game; it seemed to be his thing.

With all the regulations against magic in hockey, I could only imagine the ramifications of a demon deal, even if it was an unwilling one. They hadn't seemed to care when they thought the magic was an accident; I couldn't see how this would be much different.

But he looked so happy. Isn't that what life was all about? I wished I could've seen him when he was an angel, to see if he had that same smile—the same zest for life that emanated from him when he played hockey. Only he knew that, and only he could decide what it was worth.

I couldn't say that Burton was that bad of a guy, demon or not. No worse than many of the other supernatural beings I dealt with every day. We all had our role to play making it through life, and it seemed we were the most judgmental of others whose goals didn't match our own. It didn't make them any better, or any worse—just different.

If you thought about it, it wasn't just about Sully. His fame was a win for the team, a win for the fans, and a win for the town. So much was riding on his decision. Plus, if he now suddenly disappeared or lost all his hockey mojo at once, it might be worse than never having had it at all.

People could be ruthless when it came to their star players and the expectations they had of them. When the team was winning, it was awesome, and they were with you one-hundred percent, but if things were going badly, that really brought out the teeth and claws.

Sully was in an impossible situation.

I guess that was the price you had to pay when choosing which side of divine intervention.

19

I slumped into the overstuffed chair with a groan. My feet were singing a song of mercy after my eight-hour shift turned into twelve. I rested my arm across my eyes until the endless onslaught of neon dance lights faded from my vision and my ears stopped thumping from the music vibrations. Having heightened senses was inconvenient when working in an obnoxiously loud place.

"What's up?"

I started at my sister's voice and lifted my arm enough to get a glimpse of her questioning expression and raised brows. I hadn't heard Ava enter Gran's place. I must've been more tired than I'd realized. "Nothing."

The couch shifted as she settled to sit on the edge

of the cushion. "Nope. It's something." Not long after, a small thump announced the arrival of her cat, Savvy, on the couch. The cat's long, dark blonde hair and graceful actions mirrored Ava's down to the green almond-shaped eyes that missed nothing. Four eyes bored into me. Two human. Two feline. All disbelieving.

I received a moment's reprieve from their inquisitive stares when Mulder scrambled into the room. Like me, my Shih Tzu challenged the stereotype of the supernatural companion—and Savvy's patience. It made my dog and me a good pair. Mulder's ginormous, inquisitive eyes never judged me like the rest of the world did. He found joy in everything in his clumsy, clueless manner, which made him an adorable pet, and so far, pretty much useless as a wannabe familiar.

Jasper lingered in the hallway so he could admire Savvy from afar. Savvy was the only thing I'd found to cause Jasper to become tongue-tied.

I sat up.

"James asked about you," Ava said.

"What?"

"You know, James Stone? He asked about you while helping me out with Grace's defense," she said. "I think he might be interested in you."

I waved her off. "I'm not interested in a relation-ship with anyone now," I said more to convince myself than Ava. Although if James really was inter-ested in me, I hadn't recognized the signs. Although perhaps I couldn't see them as well since he was prac-tically transparent.

"You know what you have to do." Ava faced me and steepled her fingertips. I recognized this pose as her bracing herself to deliver a lecture.

"Why is it that so many people feel the need to tell me what I have to do? It's not up to me; it's up to Sully." My protest came out more like a whine. It was hard to take her seriously when I could see Freddie out of the corner of my eye perched on top of the bookshelf. He was trying to blend into the décor and utterly failing.

Freddie had begun popping up in the most incon-venient places. He truly was a master of disguise. Luckily, both Mulder and Savvy tolerated him. Jasper, though, seemed jealous of the attention the gargoyle was receiving.

Gran was going to love him.

"I know you won't allow Sully to make his own decision. You'll want to influence it just like you do with everything else. I hate to sound harsh, but I think you understand me when I say that you don't always have their best interest at heart." Ava ended her speech with a raised brow.

I sat up a little straighter, preparing my retort. "I agree." I allowed these two words to sink in and gain my sister's attention. "But ..."

Ava laughed. "I knew there had to be a *but*. For a minute, I thought you said that you agreed with me."

"I do, to an extent," I said. "Sully needs to make his own decision, but he needs guidance and at least a sounding board."

"Oh, and you think you're the person to do that? Since you're such a neutral party?"

"I'm the best person he's got. Joe had his own agenda, and Burton... Well, he's Burton. Who knows what he's thinking other than improving his success? I know Sully well enough to hear him out and let him weigh the pros and cons."

"There are no pros to working with Burton," Ava barked out a laugh.

"See? And you think you can be a neutral party? You've already made your decision. He has to make one that he can live with. If he's not going to be happy regaining his grace, he's never going to keep it. Or if the angels take him back and he falls again... well, I don't want to think about those consequences."

If I tried to convince him to stay, then I'd always only have a shell of him and not his true self. He would become resentful of me, and we would never be happy. He'd always wonder what would have happened if he'd made an effort to go and what it was about me that made him stay. Then he'd begin to question the things that made him stay and have doubts on whether he made the right choice. But he'd have no one to blame but me—or himself—and then, it would get ugly.

SULLY WALKED INTO THE CLUB WITHOUT HIS USUAL confident swagger.

His pace was slow. As if stalling his crossing of the room would enable him to avoid this conversation. As if I didn't already know what he had to say. As if hearing him say it, or not, would be any easier than the end result.

I knew this day would come, but I thought there would be more time. I thought everyone did, whenever there was something unsavory we wanted to delay for an hour, a minute, an eternity.

I straightened my shoulders.

I couldn't do much, but I could make this easier.

"Hi." It was all I could force out. Generally, I was unable to limit my babble, but today I could barely force the one word out.

He paused a few feet from me. "Hi." The pain filling his eyes told me that he realized I'd already determined what message he'd come to deliver.

"You don't have to say it," I said with a weak smile.

I turned toward where Burton lingered behind the bar. He gave me a little nod as if to encourage me to change Sully's mind. I shook my head and tried to shoo Burton away. He scowled but then retreated. He knew when the battle was lost, as did I. He couldn't force Sully to change his mind; he could only hope that I would.

"I do," Sully said.

"No, really. I understand. That doesn't mean I like it. I don't like it one bit, but this is bigger than me and my feelings." I busied myself with wiping the bar, avoiding looking directly at Sully.

"I didn't think you'd be this understanding," he said.

My laugh was harsh. "Believe me, neither did I." I turned to face him.

His smile was sad. "I don't want to make you turn bitter like what happened with Gloria."

"This is not like that, and I'm nothing like her." At least I hoped not. I tried to downplay the impact he had upon me, although as an angel, I'd assumed he'd be able to see right through my façade, but I could still try to hide my feelings. "Don't give yourself so much credit."

I bent as if to get something from underneath the bar when I wanted to hide the tears falling from my lashes.

I didn't have to worry about serving anyone or having them interrupt. Burton was steering any wandering customers away, still hopeful that my feminine wiles or weak, greedy heart would convince Sully to join his team. I always did like a bad boy, but asking Sully to become a demon would be extreme, and I wasn't that selfish.

Sully place his hand over mine, and my skin tingled from his touch.

"You've waited for this for hundreds of years. I think I could wait a little longer." My smile faltered.

He squeezed my hand. "That's what makes you special."

"What? Warts and all?"

He leaned forward and brushed his lips against mine for the last time. "No warts at all."

I dipped my head so he wouldn't see how it pained me to have to say goodbye. I wanted to ask if

I'd see him again, but—at the same time—I didn't want to because I feared the answer would be no.

Joe had said Sully would have to spend time redeeming himself to his superiors before he could return. I didn't know much about any of that process, but I knew that their sense of time couldn't be anything like ours.

Sully turned.

He may have blended into the crowd, or he may have just disappeared to his rightful place—wherever that was that the fallen went if they got a second chance.

A shot glass of tequila slid to a stop in front of me.

I looked up at Burton. "I'm sorry I couldn't ask him to make that sacrifice."

Burton lifted his own glass and took a sip, walking away without a word.

I stared out at the club and briefly caught the eye of a man sitting at the end of the bar. It was that same dude, Steve, who I'd chased off when he sought out Burton. He dropped his gaze when it collided with mine. I frowned as I recalled how he kept popping up like a bad penny.

A thought stirred in my brain.

Burton had said we only had a piece of the puzzle.

I strolled toward the end of the bar, snagging a

martini glass as I went. After ensuring Burton was keeping a wide berth, I mixed the martini with a bit of charm. If my hunch was right, it was time for a confession cocktail.

Steve started to get up when I approached, but I held up a hand and the martini. "Think of this as a truce. You said my martini was the best you'd ever had."

He settled back onto the bar stool. "You aren't going to chase me off again?"

I shrugged and slid my hand into my apron, hitting the record button on my phone. "Why? You made your choice." I pushed the drink toward him. "Enjoy."

He took a sip while eyeing me warily.

I lingered, filling the napkin dispenser, turning when I felt Burton's gaze boring into my back. His attention helped confirm my suspicion.

I leaned on the bar after Steve had drank almost half of the highball. "So, you are in charge of the SHL and were working with Gloria, correct?"

Steve nodded. "Yes. That didn't work out at all as planned. Once I realized Gloria wasn't going to be able to pull it off and get this demon involved," he gestured toward Burton, "I decided to try to take things into my own hands. Except you kept meddling and getting in the way."

I straightened. "I knew Gloria couldn't be the only one to blame for what happened with Grace, and then me. There's no way the SHL would put a witch in charge, with their obvious dislike of them."

"No, the SHL doesn't care too much one way or the other about witches. That was mostly Gloria. I went along with her to get what I wanted. Which she didn't deliver. Which is why I decided not to hide her identity anymore. That witch made us lose most of our employees and got us tons of bad press."

He looked at the empty martini glass with a frown, perhaps pondering what had suddenly given him the loose lips. "I didn't mean to say all that. Why did I say that?"

I clicked the recording off on my phone. "Well, it looks like you and the SHL are in for some more bad press, Steve. This time it's not just going to be the bogus SHL proceedings. This information, and how you held Grace against her will, is going to the authorities. Looks like you'll be getting your own cage in which to think about all this."

Steve began to stand, and I gestured for Burton to detain him.

Sometimes it was good to be friends with a demon.

I crossed my arms and smiled with satisfaction. Two good deeds in one day. Ava may not be the only

.one cleaning up their karma. Perhaps if I tired of being a cocktail waitress, there was a career as a private detective in my future.

I pulled out my phone and dialed. "Hi, Fran? I have a new scoop for you for the *Willow Words*."

20

I carried the hat in my hand when I entered the shop. The lights were low since the last appointment had long gone, but I knew Joe would still be around. He was usually the last one to go, and he often worked long into the night since angels had little use for sleep. "Hi, Joe."

Even with the earbuds in, Joe heard me. He turned toward me and pulled them out of his ears. The sound of muted eighties pop music drifted across to me. "How are you doing?"

Joe's question of concern threw me more than any other potential response he might've had. Joe didn't usually act concerned. He might feel that way somewhere deep inside, buried under layers of ruffles, leather, and eyeliner, but he never let it show.

Neither did I.

I nodded and thrust the hat in front of me. "I'm sorry I couldn't get you your hat back, but maybe you'll accept this one in its place. It is autographed by a short-lived hockey superstar who mysteriously disappeared."

Joe raised his brows at me. "I knew you lost it." He accepted the hat. "But I guess this might be an adequate replacement. I heard they're hard to come across."

"This one is autographed, too. Perhaps it can be your new collector's item," I said with a shrug.

He accepted the twill hat with a hint of a smile. He turned it to examine where Sully's trademark scrawl covered the hat trick hat. "Perhaps it will. I think I might like this one better. Are you sure you don't want to keep it? It should be more valuable, in more ways than one."

I shook my head.

To a hockey fan, the infamous Sully hat trick hat would be invaluable. The stories of the superstar who showed up on the hockey scene and blew everyone's mind just to disappear as quickly were bound to make headlines and would endure speculation for years to come.

The memories I held would be as special, but not visible to the public eye.

I didn't need a symbol to remind me of Sully. I

held those memories close to my heart. Besides, it wasn't goodbye forever—just for now.

"He'll be back for you. You have to have patience."

"You know that patience was never my strong point." I settled into the chair and studied my shadowy image in the mirror. It looked different in the chair and the salon with the lights down.

Joe came to stand behind me.

"Yes. But that doesn't mean that can't change. There are a lot of things that aren't set in stone, and you've grown a lot in this short time. More than you have in years." He set his hands on my shoulders and met my gaze in the mirror. "You did the right thing, Marissa. Self-sacrifice is the hardest thing to do. Maybe if the rules ever change, you'll have a chance at your own wings."

I scoffed. "I wouldn't count on those rules changing anytime soon. You angels are rigid when it comes to rules. Besides, I think there's a lot more against me than for me, when it comes to meeting standards that high."

Joe pulled out a brush and ran it through my hair. The gentle strokes soothed me more than any hug or kind words could. "You don't give yourself enough credit. I heard that you cracked the case of who's really behind the SHL. You got justice for Grace all on your own. You're becoming a regular little amateur investigator."

A frightful thought entered my mind. "This doesn't mean you're going anywhere too, does it?"

It was bad enough to lose Sully, but to lose Joe would be another blow. I didn't think I had to worry about Burton going anywhere. There was enough evil in the area to keep him busy for the next millennium.

"Don't be silly, girl. Who'd take care of your hair? Admit it, you'd be a hot mess without me." He raised a brow.

"You're right about that. One thing that's not improved, and has little hope to ever change, is my hair care spelling," I said.

"Angels might be rigid, and live by a plethora of rules, but we're not completely heartless." He pulled a coil of my hair, and it sprung back into place. "In fact, after your sacrifice, I have permission to do a freebie." He rifled through my hair to reveal the dark black streak that had been the bane of my existence lately. "I can remove this if you want."

I studied the piece that had caused me such distress, embarrassment, and frustration. It held the memory of all my mistakes and kept me on the right track to prevent me from repeating them. It was a visual reminder of the price you pay for straying from righteousness or acting impulsively.

"Nah, I think I'll keep it. It's part of my identity now. Besides, I think it makes people a little wary of me. They might wonder what I'm capable of."

Joe leaned down and met my gaze in the mirror. "How right you are." He winked. "How right you are."

"That might be the first time you've ever said I was right about anything."

"Don't get too comfortable with it. It's probably the last time." He paused. "It's a difficult price you had to pay. But that's how it works for angels. It takes sacrifice, and it's not always the angel that's sacrificing."

When he said it like that, he was trying to make me feel better, but it didn't make it any easier. I'd never let myself consider falling for someone like I did with Sully. I went against my better judgment with one too many oddballs, but they never got to know the real me.

"It's not fair," I said.

"When has life ever been fair? And if it was, would that make it better to live in a world where everything always went according to plan? No surprises, no hard work to achieve goals that were divvied out as they were seen to be fit. You, of all people, should know you would absolutely hate that. Your life is one big story, and Sully was a chapter. Can't you be happy living with that memory and knowing you gave him an even bigger gift?"

"What? My heart?"

"You let him get rid of the guilt he's carried for way too long. You let him see what it would be like to feel again and to be something in someone's eyes besides a solution to a problem, or a way to get that goal. Just as you let him see inside of you, he did the same."

I slumped in the chair. "How do you know all this?"

I knew Joe to be quick witted and an expert at hair care, but he'd never offered such a plethora of advice before. Ava would like him if she gave him a chance.

"Honey, I've been around way longer than you would believe. It took a long time, but I've learned a few things over the years." His expression saddened. "I usually don't share so much with the people dealing with my charge, but I don't like seeing you get hurt. I consider you my friend."

THREE MEN APPROACHED THE BAR. THEIR SLACK expressions indicated that they'd already indulged in a few drinks, plus they were mortal. Which meant liquor affected them quicker and more severely.

"We'll have tequilas."

Burton stood expressionless behind the bar, and at the man's request, he moved toward the shot glasses. "What kind?"

"Isn't all tequila the same? Give us whatever is cheapest." The man leaned on the bar with one elbow, swaying. The other two gazed starry-eyed at the club, confirming this was their first visit. But now these dudes had pushed one of Burton's odd buttons.

There was always one topic that opened up Burton's otherwise closed floodgates of conversation. He stilled and turned to face the men. Even though booze provided loose lips to the most sensible person, one look from him had them silenced.

The dude's expression froze, but the flicker in his eye told me he recognized that he had somehow inadvertently provoked the beast that was Burton.

He forced a chuckle to alleviate Burton's obvious irritation. "What? What did I say?"

"All the same?" Burton stared so long with his flat expression that the other two dudes stopped rubbernecking at their surroundings and turned to see what was taking so long with the shots. They both recoiled when Burton took them all in with a slow gaze. "Tequila is not all the same."

Great. I sighed and leaned against the counter. I'd be waiting a long time for my drink order to be filled. The only thing they could have done that would have been worse would be to ask for salt and a lime. The standard training wheels most felt were essential to ingest tequila instead of savoring it.

The first time I heard Burton's lesson on tequila, it had been interesting. By now, I had it memorized. Granted, a shared love of tequila was what had begun our unusual friendship, but even I could only hear so much of his obsession with educating about the merits of tequila. He felt the need to support this underdog of alcohol.

He lined up bottles on the bar to display the different types of tequila. Part of what I liked to think of as his Tequila 101. When someone who enjoyed tequila asked him for recommendations, Burton's enthusiasm might make you think he was distilling the stuff. Although, many who had seen the evil side of the cheap stuff felt that the devil himself was responsible for its inception.

By now the guys looked as if their booze buzz was wearing off, but none were brave enough to interrupt him. Terror lined their faces as if they were back in high school and didn't know what they'd done wrong but were afraid the principal would figure it out before they left the office.

It could be because Burton's demon peculiarities tended to leak out when he got irritated. This left his skin flushed and red and an angry spark in his eyes, but what was most distracting were the tips of horns that began to emerge from his head.

There were a few times I was tempted to tick him off to see if the horns would emerge the entire way, and maybe if I was lucky, there would be a tail, as well.

But even I didn't feel prepared to deal with Burton if he went full-on demon.

The horn tips were only ramping up the dudes' fear and paralyzing them from making a choice, which kept Burton's reprimand going. It was a nasty cycle, and it was only about to get worse. I decided to intervene before Burton decided to toss them to the underworld and rid them of a soul to teach them a lesson about doubting the benefits of a top shelf tequila.

I moved close enough to get within view since none of them appeared capable of looking away from Burton. Although, it wasn't the lesson they were enraptured with; it was the horns.

"Hey, Burton." I gave him my sweetest smile while also giving him my 'knock it off' stare, which he disregarded. "Maybe these guys don't know what to pick from all these tequilas." I turned to the guy closest to me and put my hand on his shoulder. He noticed me for the first time, and Burton's spell was broken. "Have you ever seen so much tequila?"

"No." The dude said to my chest. I put a finger under his chin and elevated his head until his gaze found my face. I needed him to focus if he didn't want to end up becoming one of hell's minions for insulting Burton's tequila. "Perhaps I'll recommend one of my favorites."

"Burton." I smiled, but he was already reaching for my favorite bottle of Anjou. Drinking on the job was forbidden, but Burton never told Vlad on these instances since he considered tequila education as part of the job.

He lined up four shot glasses. I reached over and added a fifth with a wink to Burton. He didn't usually have any, but from the way he looked, he needed one or things were about to get uglier than a vamp with a sunburn.

"Are you going to buy the lady a drink?" He asked the question as if it were a challenge. The sweat beading on the poor, unsuspecting guy's lip made me think he would've gladly bought me the whole bottle if Burton had asked.

After Burton poured the shots, he and I picked ours up and waited for the guys to follow suit. They did so with reluctance, their hands shaking enough to slosh the liquid around in the glass, almost spilling the tequila.

I shook my head.

If they wasted premium tequila by slopping it on the bar, they were on their own if Burton chose to make them lap it up.

I repeated a silent chant in my mind. *Don't ask for salt and a lime, don't ask for salt and a lime.*

As they lifted the shots I said, "Don't shoot it down. Just take a sip."

All three dudes looked at me as if I'd told them to chop off one of their own arms. They'd obviously intended to down the shot and get the heck out of here before Burton decided to open the gates of hell. It was the reaction most people had when they realized they were talking to a demon. That, and the bad reputation tequila had earned over the years from people indulging in too much cheap stuff. Since they remained frozen in indecision, or from fear of doing something that would enrage Burton, I intervened.

"Like this." I lifted the shot glass and held it under my nose. A slight tilt of my hand allowed me to inhale the essence. I closed my eyes, momentarily forgetting the tequila lesson I was providing and enjoying the moment. It wasn't often I could afford to enjoy my favorite tequila.

I tilted the glass to take a small sip, allowing the

liquid to sit in my mouth a moment and permeate the membranes there before swallowing. The resulting warmth pushed a sigh from me. Delicious.

An occasional taste of tequila wouldn't solve my problems, but it helped.

⚜

A WHINING SOUND DREW MY ATTENTION, AND I reached down to pull Mulder onto the bed, almost pulling my arm out of its socket in the process.

"Him too? You need to get a bigger bed." Jasper hissed and stalked further down the bed. "I would've figured out that Steve guy was involved if you'd let me get more involved in the investigation," Jasper pouted before walking in a circle and curling up on the bed.

"I'm sure you would have, but I didn't think you'd be interested since there were no more nachos involved." I raised the pillow to avoid his half-hearted swat. "I'm kidding. We do make a good team. Don't worry, next time there's a mystery to solve, or a dead body, I'll be sure to include you more."

Not that I was expecting there to be more mysteries or bodies, but who knew. I hadn't expected to be sharing a bed with a talking cat, a dog, and a gargoyle that didn't think I noticed him clinging to the bed frame, but here I was—loving it.

What's next for Marissa, Jasper, and Mulder? Find out what Mulder really thinks as he lends a paw to help with this cozy murder mystery!

I don't see dead people, but my dog does.

Magic, Mimosas & Mistletoe
A Charmed Cocktail Cozy Mystery

WILL YOU HELP OTHER READERS FIND THIS BOOK?

Thank you for reading my story! I love sharing my characters and their fun adventures. I hope they bring you as much joy reading them as they give me writing them.

If you have enjoyed this story, it would be fantastic if you would leave a review. Reviews help my books get noticed and bring them to the attention of other readers who may enjoy them.

You can leave a review for Hexes, Highballs & Hockey right here.

Have a magical day!

Maureen

paranormal species. That's what I do. I don't have a reference book. I am the reference book.

The Enchantlings Series

This Urban Fantasy story features Hope, as she struggles to determine if her ability to infuse euphoria or despair with her touch makes her the devil's spawn or his exterminator.

Other Standalone Stories

Evil Speaks Softly

They were never supposed to meet.

Fame came easily for Liv by following in the footsteps of the female writers in her family. The cycle repeated for decades...until Liv changed the story. Her villain doesn't like the revision—and he isn't a fictional character. In his story, the bad guy always wins.

Till Death

To protect an innocent man, a dutiful wife challenges her

vengeful husband...with disastrous results.

GET YOUR FREE STORIES

Get the free short stories, including, *Spells, Spirits & Stiffs*, when you sign up for my newsletter. It's free to sign up, and you can opt-out at any time. : https://www.maureenbonatch.com/free-book/

Spell, Spirits & Stiffs

What's worse than a bunch of elderly witches in provocative Halloween costumes? One dead one.

Hi, I'm Marissa Hale. I should've known that mixing cocktails, costumes, and meddling would end with a corpse.

One of the best things about living at the Willow Hill retirement condos with Gran is that Halloween is a month-long celebration. One of the worst things is that the elderly witches gorge on more gossip than treats. These magic mavens love to get the scoop, as long as they aren't the headline.

When the informant for the condo newsletter ends up dead at the Halloween party, there are more suspects than skeletons in these closets. While I'm trying to figure out whodunnit to the hostess most likely to be stabbed, the thirsty rambunctious residents raid my charmed cocktail station.

My furry sleuthing side-kicks and I might need a few tricks to ensure that things don't get even more deadly...

In case you missed it, read the story that started the adventures of Marissa, Jasper, and Mulder.

My magic might not be up to par, but I'm no killer. The question is, who is?

Curses, Cats & Corpses
A Charmed Cocktail Cozy Mystery

Do you love books, pets, and magic? Then come join my exclusive group- Must Love Magic:

https://www.facebook.com/groups/630494098126926

ABOUT THE AUTHOR

Just a small-town girl, M.L. Bonatch leads a double life. She lives in a magical world, writing cozy paranormal mysteries and sweet, humorous paranormal romance as M.L. Bonatch and urban fantasy as Maureen Bonatch.

While she's not busy writing or doing nurse things, she's a mom to her twin daughters, bicycling in the beautiful woods of PA with her hubby, doing the bidding of a feisty Shih Tzu, and dancing as much as possible. She believes music can be paired with every mood, laughter is contagious, and that caffeine and wine are essential for survival.

By signing up for her newsletter, you will be the first to learn about book sales, new releases, and other fun stuff.

Find all Maureen's stories on her website: https://www.maureenbonatch.com/

Follow her everywhere to keep up with all the magic, mystery, and mayhem.

amazon.com/-/e/B0951C41XM
bookbub.com/authors/m-l-bonatch
facebook.com/MLBonatch
instagram.com/mlbonatch.author
twitter.com/mbonatch
pinterest.com/maureenbonatch